THE CURVE OF EQUAL TIME

THE CURVE
OF EQUAL TIME

a novel

Thomas McGuire

borealbooks

Book design by Mark E. Cull

Library of Congress Cataloging-in-Publication Data

Names: McGuire, Thomas, 1945– author.
Title: The curve of equal time: a novel / Thomas McGuire.
Description: First edition. | Pasadena: Boreal Books, 2024.
Identifiers: LCCN 2024001320 (print) | LCCN 2024001321 (ebook) | ISBN 9781597099394 (paperback) | ISBN 9781597099400 (e-book)
Subjects: LCGFT: Novels.
Classification: LCC PS3613.C49965 C87 2024 (print) | LCC PS3613.C49965 (ebook) | DDC 813/.6—dc23/eng/20240130
LC record available at https://lccn.loc.gov/2024001320
LC ebook record available at https://lccn.loc.gov/2024001321

The National Endowment for the Arts, the Los Angeles County Arts Commission, the Ahmanson Foundation, the Dwight Stuart Youth Fund, the Max Factor Family Foundation, the Pasadena Tournament of Roses Foundation, the Pasadena Arts & Culture Commission and the City of Pasadena Cultural Affairs Division, the City of Los Angeles Department of Cultural Affairs, the Audrey & Sydney Irmas Charitable Foundation, the Meta & George Rosenberg Foundation, the Albert and Elaine Borchard Foundation, the Adams Family Foundation, Amazon Literary Partnership, the Sam Francis Foundation, and the Mara W. Breech Foundation partially support Red Hen Press.

First Edition
Published by Boreal Books
an imprint of Red Hen Press
www.borealbooks.org
www.redhen.org
Printed in Canada

ACKNOWLEDGMENTS

I would like to thank Peggy Shumaker at Boreal Books, who was my guardian angel throughout the long process of bringing this book to print. Also, Joeth Zucco for our friendly battles over comma placement and nautical terms. The staff at Red Hen Press were my guides in the hard work of book design and production. Thank you, Mark Cull, Kate Gale, Tobi Harper Petrie, Monica Fernandez, and especially Rebeccah Sanhueza, for your competence and courtesy.

I would like to thank Heather Lende in my home town of Haines, Alaska, for an early reading and encouragement.

A special thank you to the crew of the F/V *Aimee O*, Captain Chad Peterman, Noel Cherry, and Steve Morrell, who were my shipmates and friends for many seasons in Alaskan waters. Together we climbed mountains, hiked lonely beaches, and caught a lot of salmon. I am also in debt to many other fishing friends who provided the stories and salty language in this book.

Most of all I want to thank my family for their constant support: my wife, Sally, my children Rebecca, Rosemary, Gabriel, and Raphael, and now my seven grandchildren, who are scattered from Alaska to Kazakhstan. Together, they make my life joyful and rewarding.

THE CURVE OF EQUAL TIME

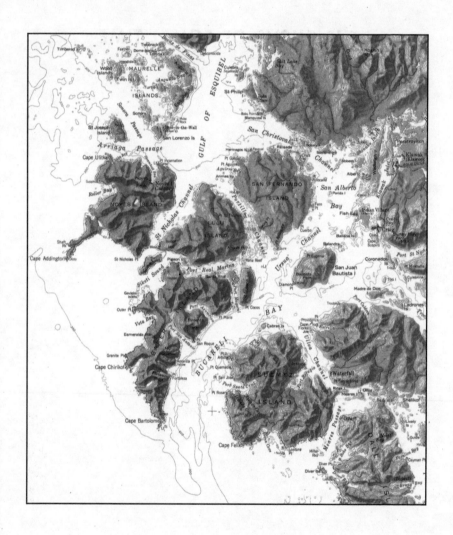

Water defines this place. Glaciers shape the mountains and mist shrouds the forest. Rain-swollen streams tumble to salt-water, where twenty-five-foot tides create a changing puzzle of rips and eddies. Wind drives the waves and generates currents that turn in a gyre as they descend through the subsurface maze of canyons and pinnacles.

The movement of the water is unfathomably complex. If something of neutral buoyancy—perhaps a human body—were to fall from the deck of a fishing boat, there would be no way to chart its descent, no way to predict its final resting place.

Understanding what caused the fall might also be difficult.

CHAPTER 1

Ketchikan (55.20.5'N., 131.38.7'W.) on the SW
side of Revillagigedo Island and on the E side
of Tongass Narrows . . . is 659 miles from Seattle
via the inside passage.

—*US Coast Pilot*

A gust of wind and rain tilted the *Emma Rose* as she came alongside the transient float. From the bow, Nora Tyler tossed a mooring line to a deckhand who had jumped onto the dock. She passed her end through the hawse hole and fastened it to a cleat, then walked back to the galley, picked up her sea bag, and climbed over the rail.

"Where the hell you think you're going?" the skipper Larry yelled from the pilothouse window, but Nora headed landward without looking back. Mussels coated the dock pilings, and the exposed mud smelled rank. The harbor ramp slanted steeply to the street. Why was it always low tide and raining wherever she came ashore?

There was a telephone booth near the top of the ramp. Nora called the ferry terminal to check the scheduled sailings and then called her cousin Steve at the cannery in Petersburg.

"Nora," Steve answered warily. "Where are you?"

"Ketchikan."

"We figured you'd be here by now. What's up?"

Nora waited two beats. "I thought the job was for a cook, not a concubine."

"Uh-oh," Steve said. "Pretty bad?"

"Yup."

"Sorry about that. Not much I can do. We just hire the tenders, sign a contract. It's his boat."

"I know, I know. But I gotta find something else. Do you know of anything?"

"I'll check around. How are you going to get here?"

"There's a ferry tonight."

"So you'd be here, what, late tomorrow? Well, call me when you get in."

Nora thought she heard a sigh as Steve hung up. How many favors could you ask of a second cousin whom you scarcely knew?

Passing cars tore sheets of water from the pavement. Nora considered calling her daughter in Phoenix, but Trish had probably left for her hospital job by now, which meant her boyfriend, Duane, might answer the phone, the last voice Nora wanted to hear.

She shouldered her sea bag and started to walk toward town, stopping on the bridge over Ketchikan Creek to look at the forest of masts and rigging in the crowded harbor. Twenty years since she had crewed on a fish boat, maybe that wasn't long enough, but at least she was back in Alaska. Home—the place where, when you had to run, they had to let you hide. As Joe Louis and Robert Frost almost said.

Three hours later, Nora sat on a barstool, nursing a margarita to kill time till the ferry's scheduled departure. After her voyage on the *Emma Rose*, she did not want to board another boat till the last possible moment. A nearby window overlooked Bar Point Basin, and she watched a troller approach the dock, coming in fast at a bad angle and then backing down hard. A guy in a green jacket ran out of the wheelhouse and flung a line toward the dock. A passerby grabbed it and helped avert disaster.

Green jacket appeared to be the only one onboard. When the boat was secure, he jumped ashore and said something to his rescuer, who laughed aloud and slapped him on the back. A comedian, Nora figured.

The boat was a Cape Fairweather troller almost identical to the *Nora Ann*, the boat Nora and her ex-husband, Buck, had fished back when the world was young. Which may have been why Nora spoke to the guy when he walked into the bar and sat down two barstools away. The back of his green jacket read "Shamrock Bar / Libby, Montana."

Above the front breast pocket, "Nick" was embroidered in yellow thread. He ordered a beer.

"Hoochies," Nora said to him.

"Beg your pardon?"

"Hoochies, her earrings. You were staring at them."

"Oh, yeah." The guy looked again at the barmaid's squiggly purple earrings.

"They're killer coho bait, hoochies," said Nora, but how could someone own a troller and not know this?

"But . . . fluorescent purple? There's nothing like that in the ocean, is there?"

"Who knows?" Nora figured humans were not the only creatures entitled to bad taste and poor judgment.

Nick gave her a polite elevator look, head to toe and back. "May I?" he asked, indicating Nora's nearly empty glass.

Nora looked at the clock above the bar. Time was dragging; there was still more than an hour till she needed to be at the terminal. She was bored, as well as broke, and the guy had said both "beg your pardon" and "may I" in a two-minute conversation, which was more courtesy than Buck had shown in ten years of marriage.

"I shouldn't, but, yeah, thank you," she said. Nick signaled the barmaid and then moved across to sit beside her. Nora hoped this would not turn out to be a bad idea.

"I watched you land your boat," she said.

Nick flinched at the memory. "I'm kind of a rookie. Just brought her up from Seattle. Long trip."

"How long?"

"Three weeks."

"Three weeks? Ouch."

"First I got in trouble at Campbell River, the straits there?"

"Seymour Narrows."

"Right. I got spun around in the tide rips and then almost run down by this huge cruise ship. Like a floating apartment building. Some idiotic name—*Crystal Harmony*?"

"I've seen her." Nora remembered the *Crystal Harmony* in Grenville

Channel, lit up like a social climber's wedding cake. "But didn't you check the current tables?"

"The what?"

"Never mind."

"Then the very next day—"

"I don't get it," Nora interrupted. Back in her fishing days, she had listened to way too many litanies of boat disasters. "How did you end up owning a troller? You don't seem like a boat person."

"This guy, Mitch, made it sound like you could pick money off the beaches up here. A fishing vacation with pay."

"And you met Mitch where?"

"The Shamrock Bar, back in Montana. I was part owner."

Nora looked at his hands, callused and weather-beaten. He had done other things than tend bar.

"I did construction mostly," Nick had noticed her glance, "and farm-work, but then I blew my savings on a half share of the Shamrock. Only turns out running a bar wasn't the lark I thought it would be. I was looking for a way out when Mitch shows up and I trade him my share of the bar for his boat, straight across."

"Oh, brother." Nora shook her head. Why did she always run into these losers? But the guy had an offbeat charm, like a lost dog that shows up at your door. She looked at the clock and quickly drained her glass.

"One more?" Nick asked.

"Gotta run. Another time, maybe." As if. Nora picked up her sea bag and pulled out her pocket watch to double-check the time, then froze in disbelief. The hands said seven, not six. She looked at the bar clock again, then back at her watch.

"The owner doesn't believe in Daylight Savings," the barmaid said, seeing Nora's confusion. "Kind of a local joke. Guys use it as an excuse with their wives." She shrugged.

Lord God, no. Nora ran to the window and looked down Tongass Narrows. The terminal was around a bend, but in her mind's eye she could see the ferry, ablaze with lights, disappearing north like another lost opportunity.

The next northbound ferry was three days away. Nora walked slowly back to her barstool. Nick raised his hand and made a circular motion to the barmaid. A fresh margarita quickly appeared. Nora grabbed it and gulped.

"Problems?" Nick asked.

"I need a ride to Petersburg."

Two hundred miles north, Danny Sullivan lit a cigarette on the back deck of the *Viking Hero*. A salmon jumped nearby. A dozen seine boats lay at anchor in Cosmos Cove, waiting for the fishing to begin the next day. All the boats were familiar to Danny, though their crews changed every year.

Danny could see the *Hero's* skipper, Sven, up in the wheelhouse, talking to someone on the single sideband radio. No doubt Sven was thinking about making a move; very few salmon were showing in the bay. The only other area open to fishing was District 4, the outside waters, which would require a nightlong run down Chatham Strait. Danny figured there were not enough fish this early in the season to justify the effort, but Sven was a restless soul.

Danny looked up at the saw-toothed mountains of Baranof Island. The snowfields held the last of the sunlight. Danny wished he were somewhere else entirely, someplace not so hard-edged, but the rumble of the *Hero's* main engine brought him back to reality. Sven came out of the wheelhouse and, without a word, jerked his thumb upward in peremptory fashion.

"Shit," Danny said as he tossed his cigarette overboard and headed to the bow to raise the anchor.

Sven opened the throttle before Danny had the anchor fully secured. The *Hero's* wake bounced the other boats as she left the cove. Back in the galley, Danny found the cook, Melody, playing solitaire while the dishes sat unwashed in the sink. She snuck a black queen out from under the pack and placed it on a red king. Then moved a red jack onto the queen.

"Cheating? At solitaire?" Danny tried to make it sound like a joke.

"Fuck off, Daniel." Melody turned three more cards without looking up.

Danny shrugged and headed for the fo'c'sle. The *Viking Hero* was a whaleback design, with the fo'c'sle just forward of the galley and on the same level. This was a convenient layout, but the resultant absence of windows made the galley dark and unwelcoming and gave the boat ungainly lines to Danny's mind. He kicked off his boots and rolled into his bunk. In the opposite berth, Aaron was reading a magazine called *Combat Handguns*. The other crewman, Billy Nichols, must have taken the first wheel watch. Aaron would be next, which meant four hours till Danny's own watch, the longest stretch of sleep he could expect for this opening, maybe for the entire season. He closed his eyes.

Faceless beings chased Danny down endless corridors with no exit. A rough hand shook him awake. "Five minutes," Aaron said.

Danny rubbed his eyes to clear the cobwebs, then put on his boots and headed for the galley. As he poured a mug of coffee, he heard a low voice from Sven's stateroom followed by a muffled laugh. Danny looked toward the fo'c'sle; Melody's bunk was empty. Danny shook his head and headed up the stairs to the flying bridge.

"What the fuck's Sven thinking?" Aaron bitched. He was bent over the logbook, signing off his watch. "Fuckin' chasin' radio fish. He wanted to fish Noyes, why didn't he just head there in the first place?"

"Ain't our call, bro."

Aaron headed down the companionway, still grumbling. What a sorehead. Back in prison, even the Chicano gangs had left him alone.

At least the wheelhouse was peaceful and dark, aside from the faint green glow of the radar. The *Hero* was running on autopilot, which meant Danny was more watchman than helmsman. He scanned the radar for other traffic. There was a big blip on the Baranof side, probably an inbound log ship. Nothing else. He reached overhead to the VHF radio and switched to the Coast Guard weather channel. "Outside waters, Dixon Entrance to Cape Fairweather," the metallic voice said. "Winds southeast variable to fifteen, switching to southwest twenty-five. Seas three feet, building to six feet. Outlook, southwest thirty, seas to eight feet."

Not too enticing. The Point Crowley light was a long way ahead, but the boat already rolled to the bite of the open ocean. Looking aft Danny saw Melody standing at the rail, a shadowy figure in the faint light from the galley door. She was hugging herself as if cold, her shoulders bowed. Not too long ago, Melody had been Danny's girlfriend. Sharing the skipper's bunk might be a step up, but if Melody thought that would cut her any slack, she sure didn't know Sven.

Danny checked the radar and compass and changed the course two degrees west. What he needed was a major change of course himself. With luck, this might be his last year as a deckhand. One big score and he could kiss this life goodbye.

Ever since high school, Danny had dealt a little weed, what's the problem? But when he tried to move some harder stuff with the crab fleet out of Dutch Harbor, he had gotten in over his head with some very hard guys. Then a stupid sale in a Seattle bar earned him a stint in state prison.

Aaron Dobbs had been his cellmate in Walla Walla, and he had a source for pills—black beauties, reds, bennies—and other product as well. Danny had convinced Aaron there was a big market in the fishing fleet, and they decided to go partners. Problem was, they needed money upfront, and Danny had talked Sven into bankrolling the operation. Having Sven and Aaron in on the same deal was worse than having two bulls in one china shop. And now Mano, Danny's contact in Dutch Harbor, was trying to get a piece of the action. Some bullshit claim about Danny owing him money.

No more dealing, once this summer was over, Danny promised himself. He looked down at the white roll of the bow wave on the face of the dark water.

Around about midnight, Nick and Nora left the bar. Nick insisted on carrying her bag but almost fell on the slippery ramp. Nora grabbed his right arm and together they navigated the docks. She had chased the margaritas with a couple of beers, and her free hand still held a bottle. Going home with a stranger was a risk Nora had not taken in years, but with fifty bucks and a maxed-out credit card in her purse, what choice did she have?

Nick was singing softly, something about one for my baby and one more for the road. Nora recognized the song—Sinatra, maybe? Two herring gulls standing on a boat rail took flight rather than join the chorus.

Nick's troller had weathered paint and frayed rigging; she had seen hard days. Nora felt a sudden knell of memory, a blurred image of the *Nora Ann* tied to the Point Baker dock in a heavy fog. *Guinevere* was painted on the bow of Nick's boat. *Guinevere?* Wasn't that the name of the girl Buck had in tow the last time he visited Nora and Trish? Little twit in a black turtleneck, claimed she went to Reed College? In a pig's ear, Reed College.

Nora had a sudden drunken insight that the *Guinevere* actually was the *Nora Ann*, the name changed one more time to change the boat's luck. But what would change her own luck? Her fate? Nora flung her beer bottle at the *Guinevere's* bow. Brown glass broke as though the boat was being launched again.

"Hey," Nick said.

CHAPTER 2

*Snow Passage is between Bushy Island, the
northernmost of the Kashevarof group, and
Zarembo Island. It is a deep channel with foul
shores and strong tidal currents.*

—*US Coast Pilot*

The wake of a passing boat woke Nora. She sat on the edge of the *Guinevere*'s daybed and searched through her handbag till she found two aspirin that she swallowed dry. The fo'c'sle was three steps down and forward. She could see Nick lying face down on a bunk, still passed out. At least he had been a gentleman about the sleeping arrangements.

The galley had a continuously burning oil stove, and Nora moved the kettle to the hot spot. When the water boiled, she made a pot of coffee and took a cup outside. The bitter taste fit her mood. She dreaded calling Cousin Steve. Her excuse about the clock would sound so lame. Never before had she missed a ferry. Nor an airplane, train, taxi. Never been late for work. What message were the gods sending? And why choose Nick as their messenger?

Where was Nick headed? He had been vague about his destination and relieved to have Nora aboard as far as Petersburg. Nora looked at the *Guinevere*'s trolling cockpit and its gurdies. Did Nick even know how to run the gear? Did he have any idea how difficult it was to catch fish? Buck had spent two boyhood summers fishing on a troller off the Oregon coast. Even with this bit of experience, their first season on the *Nora Ann* had been a constant knot of frustration, anger, fear—with occasional moments of exuberance and laughter, she had to admit.

Nora had met Buck during the Wrangell Fourth of July festival the year she turned eighteen. That was also the year the first combat troops were sent to Viet Nam; a time of bad beginnings and troubled outcomes.

Buck had come to town from one of the outlying camps to enter the logging contests. In the final of the logrolling competition, when his opponent fell, Buck leaped in the air, clicked his caulked heels together, and with a loud whoop fell in the harbor himself. His tin piss-pot hardhat floated free, and he hauled himself up on the dock and stood soaking wet and laughing, powerful as a young sea lion. Nora was standing in the crowd of spectators but edged closer, trying to catch Buck's eye. Unfortunately, the ploy worked. Six months later, they were married, and five months after that, Trish was born.

For five years, they moved from logging camp to logging camp. Always another trailer sitting on a bulldozed pad in the forest. Always the rusted machinery, the incessant rain, the endless camp gossip. Buck was a competent logger, but he was never in camp long before he wanted to fight the foreman. Or chase someone's wife. When there were no more bridges to burn, Buck persuaded Nora's parents to take a second mortgage on their home so he could buy a troller.

Trolling had proved no better. Buck never stayed in one place long enough to learn the drags. They bounced from Noyes Island to Point Baker to Icy Strait, chasing the dream of one big season, but their mountain of debt never grew smaller. In Nora's memory, she was the one who ran the gear, cooked, and took care of Trish while Buck chatted on the radio. Twice she left and twice she came back. The second time, there was a young girl working as Buck's puller, and Buck wanted to keep them both on the boat. A week of that was enough. Nora moved to Seattle and filed for divorce. Her portion of the settlement was a share of the boat debt.

Hard to believe Buck was seven years gone now, drowned on the Columbia Bar. He had been crabbing with some old high school buddy. One last fling at the moon in one last decrepit boat.

Jennifer, she suddenly remembered. That had been the name of Buck's last piece of fluff, not *Guinevere*.

"Morning," Nick said. He stood in the galley door, coffee cup in hand, smiling. Nora realized she did not even know his last name.

On the western side of Noyes Island, steep seas broke against a cliff of black basalt. Just offshore, the *Viking Hero* rolled wickedly in the trough as her net came aboard with very few fish. Sven cut the towing bridle free, and Danny cranked the skiff's wheel hard over and headed for the stern of the big boat.

Billy reached down, grabbed the skiff's painter, and hooked it to the skiff release. Aaron winched it taut. Danny climbed aboard and crossed the net pile. He stripped off his rain jacket and entered the galley. They had fished hard all morning, and Melody had not bothered to send any food out to the skiff. Midafternoon now, Danny was cold, hungry, and irritable. Melody sat at the galley table in her raingear, head bowed as though she was crying. While stacking gear in the morning, Billy had lost control of one of the purse line rings, and it had smacked Melody in the face. Even with her head down, Danny could see the beginning of a pretty good shiner.

The coffee pot was empty. Danny took a jar of instant coffee from the cupboard, spooned some into his mug, then filled it with hot water from the tap. He grimaced at the taste. He opened the refrigerator, holding the door with his knee against the boat's motion. Slim pickings. He stuck two apples in his pocket, grabbed a leftover pork chop, tore the meat free with his teeth, and flung the bone out the window. The engine growled as Sven kicked the boat in gear. Danny grabbed his mug and rain jacket and raced for the skiff. The *Hero* began to turn, the way Sven always did at the beginning of a set, a wolf circling its prey.

The *Hero* fished till 8:00 p.m. and then headed for town. Melody had worked with manic energy throughout the afternoon. Danny figured she had upped the amperage of whatever pills she was taking, but if she went from so low to so high on such a steep gradient, the ultimate crash could be ugly. The roller coaster from hell.

At the galley table, Sven bitched that his steak was overdone and his baked potato raw in the middle. Melody answered with a taunt about the amount of fish they had caught. Sven flared up and threw the contents of his plate out the door and stormed up to the wheelhouse.

Fuckin' Sven, always on the rag. He had gone through a messy divorce in the winter. He had lost his house and then had to double his boat loan to pay cash for his wife's share. These days Sven was like a bull Danny had seen in Barcelona on his one trip abroad. The picadors had lanced the bull to bring his head down, but the bull stood his ground in the middle of the arena, snorting blood, his legs braced, his eyes mean. A good time to be way back in the cheap seats.

Danny finished his meal and headed for his bunk. An hour later, he awoke with a burning need to piss. He limped barefoot through the galley. Melody was washing dishes and chattering like a magpie to Aaron who stood close behind her, drinking a beer. As Danny passed by, Aaron trailed a hand down Melody's back to rest on her rump.

Uh-oh, Danny thought, afraid that the summer was about to become even more complicated.

The *Guinevere* had left Ketchikan earlier that afternoon. After a bumpy ride in Clarence Strait, she anchored for the night behind Rookery Island at the north end of Snow Passage, a spot Nora remembered from the old days. It was poor holding ground, but Nick had only a generic cruising guide, and Nora told him it would be foolhardy to attempt Wrangell Narrows in the dark without a proper chart.

Not far from the *Guinevere*, a humpback whale jumped clear of the water, then jumped again, a shallow arc of flight followed by an explosion of spray that sparkled in the evening light. Always whales in Snow Passage, Nora thought, some things never changed.

Being on a small fish boat after so many years felt both familiar and strange to her—like visiting a house where you once lived, or meeting an old boyfriend and remembering the lines of his body, the touch of his hands.

Nick came up from the engine room, wiping his hands on an oily rag. "I dunno," he said. "I added two quarts of oil this morning but she just took three more."

"That better be enough to get us to Petersburg," said Nora. Beyond that she did not care.

CHAPTER 3

The Eye Opener is a rocky ledge in the middle of
Sumner Strait, about 11.7 miles E of Pt. Baker.
It is marked by The Eye Opener Light . . . shown
from a skeleton tower on a brown cylindrical
base with a red and white diamond-shaped daymark.
　　　　　　　　　　　　　　　　　—US Coast Pilot

The morning sun had just cleared the mountains when Nick hit the starter button. An ominous clanging came from the *Guinevere's* engine, but the sound quickly smoothed and the exhaust rumbled politely in the stack.

Nora took the wheel and set a course for the entrance to Wrangell Narrows. Ten minutes later the clanging from the engine returned, louder. Nick crossed glances with Nora, then looked at the gauges. No oil pressure.

"Jesus," Nick said. He shut down the main and headed for the tiny engine room. Nora poked her head down after him. She could see that the bilge and the bulkhead were dark with sprayed oil. Nick was on his knees, studying the problem. Nora could see his lips moving, but she figured he wasn't praying. Then again, maybe he was.

"Blew the rear seal," he said when he climbed back out. "Or maybe worse. Maybe the whole goddamn engine. Think we should call the Coast Guard?"

"I wouldn't. Not yet. I heard seiners on the radio coming back from an opener. One of them will give us a tow."

"Seiners?"

"Salmon fishermen, like us. Only bigger boats, bigger crews, bigger egos." And more money, Nora thought. Growing up in Wrangell, she had always thought gear group animosities were foolish, but then she started trolling and resentment of the bigger boats became a fact of life.

She and Nick went out on deck and looked around. A few gillnetters were fishing west of them, near Point Baker, but there were no boats closer by. Nick pulled a thin cigar from his pocket and studied it meditatively.

"This guy, Mitch," Nora said, "he offers to sell you anything else, you might want to think about it first."

Nick lit his cigar and blew a plume of smoke. "Well, at this very moment Mitch is probably in the basement of the Shamrock checking out the leaky plumbing. Unless he's upstairs mopping up spilled beer and vomit, trying to figure out if the barmaid's been dipping in the till."

Nick looked at the sun-spangled water and forested hills, glanced at Nora, and burst out laughing.

Danny was on the wheel when the Viking Hero rounded Point Baker. Gillnetters worked the tide rips there, and Danny clicked off the autopilot to weave the Hero through the maze of nets. He watched one fisherman wind his net on the drum, the meshes glistening in the morning sun. The guy picked a single salmon and tossed it in the hold. Danny waved, but the guy did not acknowledge it. Sometimes Danny thought of buying a gillnet permit and a boat he could work alone. Avoid all the crew hassles. But it took money to get started, and no bank would ever underwrite a loan, given his record, both credit and criminal.

The *Hero* passed the Eye Opener, the lonely buoy marking a pinnacle in the middle of Sumner Strait. Not far ahead, Danny saw a troller drifting, obviously dead in the water. He picked up the binoculars and looked at the boat. The *Guinevere*, not a name he knew.

"*Viking Hero, Viking Hero*, this is the *Guinevere*." A woman's voice came from the VHF.

Danny keyed the mike, "This is the *Viking Hero*, WSV 4583, back to the call. Got a problem there, cap?"

"Yeah, this is the *Guinevere*. We've got engine trouble, any chance you can help?"

"Whaddaya need?"

"Well," the voice hesitated, "how about a tow into Petersburg?"

"Be right there," Danny said and signed off.

"The fuck's goin' on?" Sven said from behind him. Danny had throttled back as he talked to the *Guinevere*, and the change in engine noise had brought Sven instantly from his bunk. He was bare-chested, and his belly hung over the band of his sweatpants.

"Troller broke down. Needs a tow in."

"Fuckin' amateurs." Sven scratched his belly and looked out the window at the wounded *Guinevere*. Sven had heavy shoulders and a bull neck. His blond hair was thinning on top, but his chest was heavily furred. He picked up the tide book and studied it, then looked at his watch, thinking of the Narrows. "Slack tide at the mouth, but we'll be bucking the flood at the far end. Shit. Well, you better get a line ready."

"*Viking Hero?*" Nick raised his eyebrows at the name.

"Typical Petersburg."

"I thought you were from Petersburg."

"Wrangell. It's different." The towns were barely thirty miles apart but on separate islands. That thirty miles made a difference. At least it had, once upon a time, and a very long time ago that was.

The *Viking Hero* slowed and turned alongside. A heavyset man came out of the wheelhouse and looked down at them. He was shirtless and wore sweatpants with the words "Dutch Harbor" in big block letters down the legs. "What's the problem?" he asked.

"Engine blew," Nick said.

The man shrugged and went back into the wheelhouse without another word.

A thin, bearded guy stood on the back deck, grinning at them as he held a coil of heavy line. "Hey, shit happens," he yelled and threw Nick one end of the line. "You wanna put that on your bow cleat, cap?"

While they rigged the towline a woman wearing shorts and a T-shirt came out on the deck of the *Viking Hero*. She brushed her long hair as she stared at Nick and Nora. She gathered the hair in one hand, let it fall free, then tossed her head and began to brush again. Putting on a show, Nora thought, but who was the intended audience? Even at a distance she thought she could see black roots beneath the blonde hair, crow's feet around the eyes. One of those eyes was blackened. Someone, Nora thought, who needed no introduction to life's little disappointments.

Nick was also watching the woman out of the corner of his eye. Nora resisted the temptation to put an elbow in his ribs. As the *Hero* got underway, the bearded guy paid out about ten fathoms of line and made it fast. The line drew taut and he gave Nick and Nora a thumbs-up.

"Somebody better watch the wheel, even if she is just a hulk," Nora said and went back inside and sat in the captain's chair.

The VHF crackled to life. "This is the tug *Robert A. Foss* southbound in Wrangell Narrows with a barge in tow. Any concerned traffic please respond."

"'Concerned traffic.'" Nick stood beside Nora now. "Now there's a concept they could have used on the Edsel Ford Expressway, back in Detroit."

Always the wisecracks with Nick, but Nora could tell he was hurting inside. "So what are you gonna do in Petersburg?" she asked.

"See what it costs to get it fixed. However much is too much. Guess I'll have to look for work."

"Another dream gone bust."

"It wasn't a dream, just something I stumbled into."

"Come on, Nick. Somewhere, sometime, you must have had a dream."

Nick was silent for a moment, then said, "Baseball."

"Baseball?"

"What's wrong with that?"

"I was hoping for something a little more . . . grown up?"

"But, baseball—" Nick started, then stopped. There were some things you knew were true but could never explain. "All I ever wanted, growing up, was to play in the big leagues. That's all. Only it didn't work out."

"How close did you get?"

"That close." Nick held out a thumb and forefinger. Then he remembered the long bus rides, the cheap motels, the run-down stadiums with empty bleacher seats. "Naah," he said quietly. "I was miles away. Miles. I was a star in high school and college, then kicked around the minors a few years. Got as high as the A league, but that's a long way from the bigs, truth be told."

"So what happened?" Nora asked.

"I hurt my shoulder playing third. The manager wouldn't let me sit down and wait for it to heal. I went one for forty-one and got released."

"And that was it? You never tried anything else?"

"Not really. I bummed my way out West and started doing farm-work. Following the harvest, you know? Me and the Mexicans."

"Doesn't sound too lucrative."

"Enough for a cheap room and a jug of wine, most days. I was picking apples near Spokane when I heard there was work on the Libby Dam, so I joined the Laborers' Union. After the dam ended I just stayed with the union. When they started the Alaska pipeline, I worked out of the Fairbanks local for four years. Made a ton of money and went on, like, a yearlong drunk. Then bought a share of the bar I woke up in."

Nora started to make a tart reply but stopped short. Was Nick's story that much different from her own? For twenty years as a single mom she had worked dead-end jobs in Seattle, two jobs at once when Trish was in nursing school. Her last job had been at a Valu-Mart in Kent. She had walked off mid-shift after a meaningless argument with the assistant manager, then started looking for a way back to Alaska. Her few belongings were in a storage unit. She had a little money in the bank but no health insurance, no retirement plan. Had she ever even had a dream?

They were in the Narrows now, passing the entrance to Duncan Canal. Patches of fog still clung to the gullied hillsides and there was a narrow strip of beach like a selvage edge. Nora remembered there was a centuries-old Russian cannon somewhere in this stretch, visible only on the minus tides. A barnacle-clad symbol of all things left behind.

CHAPTER 4

Petersburg is a fishing center on Mitkof
Island, on the E side of Wrangell Narrows,
1 mile inside the N entrance.

—US Coast Pilot

Rain fell in tent city. Toby MacGregor rolled over and flung out his arm, but Sara was not there. Toby sat up and poked his head through the tent flaps. In the faint light, the bright nylon tents could have been exotic mushrooms. Beneath a lean-to fashioned from blue tarps, a figure shrouded in a mummy bag moved restlessly.

Toby lay back on his sleeping bag and listened to the rain. A mosquito droned inside the tent, and he watched a drop form on the tent wall and fall into a small puddle. That had been his side of the tent till Sara had found work at the Petersburg cannery and moved into their dormitory. Her departure had not been friendly, but at least now he could stretch his bedroll on the high side. Toby closed his eyes and thought about the day ahead—walking the docks yet again, looking for work.

After an hour of restless turning, he decided to hitchhike to town. He could get coffee at the Homestead and then pound the docks. As he left his tent the sky began to clear. The seine fleet was due in from the outer coast this morning. Maybe, just maybe, a boat would need a new deckhand.

Fish came up the chute from the pump and splashed on the sorting table. Nora grabbed a sockeye and flipped it into the totes behind her. Next to her, a kid wearing a Seahawks cap picked up a fish and looked at it dubiously. "Coho," Nora said and the kid threw the fish into the appropriate tote. At least Nora could tell the five species of salmon apart, unlike the college kids who worked alongside her.

This was Nora's fourth day of work. Her cousin Steve had been unable to find her a job with another tender, and the only thing left was cannery work, a bit of a comedown. Now she was part of the beach crew, so called because they were the first to handle the fish coming off the boats.

The banging of aluminum totes and the high whine of the forklift blended with the incessant blare of rock music from the boombox on a table next to the scales. Nora remembered winter weekends when she was in high school, picking shrimp at the Reliance cannery with a gaggle of mostly older ladies. It was always cold in the cannery and quiet, save for the incessant hum of gossip. Picking shrimp was almost like a quilting circle, nothing like this mad hurdy-gurdy.

A tall Asian girl in a Stanford sweatshirt manned the scales. She marked the weight and pulled a lever that sent the pink salmon down to another belt, bound for the slime line where they would be gutted and headed.

A forklift removed a full tote of sockeye, and the Asian girl slammed an empty one in its place. Sara Quan, that was her name. She was fast and surprisingly strong but too stuck up for Nora's taste. The Seahawks kid, Eric, had tried to chat her up during the morning coffee break, but Sara had brushed him off like Cleopatra using a whisk on a particularly inconsequential housefly.

The boat they were unloading was the *Viking Hero*, back from another one-day opening on the outer coast. Not all the fleet had gone west. There was a midweek opening at the Hidden Falls hatchery, and many of the boats had already headed north. Nora figured that the *Viking Hero*, once unloaded, would run all night to make that opener. That would mean another sleepless night for the *Hero*'s crew; Sven Oslund was a hard driver.

The fish pump's hose came out of the *Hero*'s hold blowing foam. The two cannery workers on the float dropped the suction end into the saltwater and cycled the pump again to clear it. The last few fish splashed onto the sorting table in a flurry of foam and seawater.

The beach crew broke for lunch. Nora quickly stripped off her apron and gloves and took her paper bag to a bench in the sun. Ahead of her Sara Quan crossed the street, headed for the dorm. A lanky, redheaded kid called to her, but she put her head down and ran up the dormitory stairs. Nora remembered the kid accompanying Sara to work her first morning. He had an easy grin but watchful eyes. He looked like a keeper to Nora but apparently not to Ms. Quan.

Nora peeled an orange and looked at the gulls that crowded the cannery roofs like an early fall of snow. On the shadowed side of the cold storage building, she could see Eric talking with the tall, straggly-haired deckhand from the *Viking Hero*. Aaron, she thought his name was. Something passed between the two. What was that all about? Better not to know.

After her shift ended, Nora decided to visit the harbor. When she and Nick had tied up the *Guinevere*, Nora had left without a backward glance. She had enough troubles of her own. However, she had found no one in Petersburg she could talk with. Cousin Steve was busy with his job and his young family. Her few friends from long ago were similarly involved, and her coworkers were so young they were like a different species. At least Nick could commiserate with her.

The *Guinevere* had moved to the back of the harbor alongside the other derelicts. Behind her was a Chris-Craft cabin cruiser with sun-bleached mahogany trim and plywood patches over rotting planking. The letters *HT* were painted clumsily on the cabin, a sign that it had once been a hand troller. Rafted outside the cruiser was a sailboat with dead houseplants on the cabin roof and a faded For Sale sign. It also bore the *HT* stigma. Both boats had moss growing along their waterlines, the marine equivalent of five o'clock shadow.

The *Guinevere* had a padlock on her door. Nora peeked through the window. The galley was clean, but she could tell the stove was not lit. Where was Nick?

Feeling blue, Nora walked to the end of the dock. In the Narrows, a red nun buoy tilted hard over, caught in the current's grip.

CHAPTER 5

Kasnyku Bay, on the W. side of Chatham
Strait about 14 miles NW of Point Gardner,
has deep water and no secure anchorage.

—*US Coast Pilot*

The net snaked over the stern of the *Lily Langtry*. Nick watched the skiff tow the net in a long arc that curved back toward the *Lily*. The boys had said this was going to be a round haul, whatever that meant.

The skiff was a blocky aluminum boat with a big diesel inboard engine that was both loud and dirty. The last of the net slipped off the *Lily*'s stern and the towline came taut just as the skiff came alongside. The skiff man, Marcus, threw a coiled line to Nick who threaded it through the purse block and then took three wraps around the forward drum of the deck winch, as he had been coached to do. Once the winch was turning, Marcus popped the pelican hook, freeing the skiff from the seine. He opened the throttle and made a tight turn around the *Lily*'s stern, beneath the seine's towline. George pulled the Canadian release that secured the wing end of the purse line, then brought the line forward and rove it through the second purse block that swung from the starboard davit and brought it to the deck winch.

This was all a confused blur to Nick, a square dance in a madhouse. He had no idea which piece of gear did what, nor what their names signified. The three other deckhands had given Nick a long chalk talk the night before, laughing at his complete lack of what they considered common knowledge. Marcus had done most of the talking, and Nick gathered that a skiff man's responsibilities made him a sort of first mate.

From this talk, Nick remembered not much. He knew that the net was about a quarter mile long and seventy feet deep. It had a cork line at the top, a weighted lead line on the bottom, and strips of web in between. The purse line that closed the net ran through bronze rings fastened by bridles to the lead line. Nick's principal job would be stacking the lead line and rings as they hauled the net.

Now he flaked down his end of the purse line, laying loops one way and then another, watching George out of the corner of his eye. George worked almost casually, a cigarette dangling from his mouth, but his pile was perfectly neat and square while Nick struggled to keep up with the line as it fell from the drum in a coil as sinuous as a cobra.

When the net was fully pursed, the gathered rings appeared in a bunch at the starboard rail and Nick shut down the winch. George took a curved metal bar he called the bacon hook, threaded it through the rings, then clipped a cable to it. The skipper, Buddy, had come down from the flying bridge. Sixty feet away on the port side, Marcus side-towed with the skiff to keep the *Hero* clear of her own net. With Buddy at the winch, they lifted the rings above the rail. George pulled the tail end of the purse line free of the rings and motioned Nick to follow him to the back deck.

"Here's where the work starts, partner," George said with a snaggle-toothed grin. Long, unkempt hair struggled from beneath his sou'wester hat. He wore a dark green Helly Hansen jacket and ragged yellow rain pants that were patched with duct tape.

Hanging from a gooseneck on the boom above them was a hydraulically driven block with a rubber-coated sheave the size of a car tire. George grabbed the rope dangling from it and, with Nick's help, hauled on the line till the wing end of the seine began to spill over the power block. George began to lay the cork line in tiered loops on the port side while Pete stacked the web in the middle and Nick coiled the lead line along the starboard rail. Whenever Nick came to a purse ring, he would slam it onto a bar mounted on the starboard rail. The skipper stood directly behind the wheelhouse running the block from a remote switch. Three times that first set, Nick dropped a purse ring, and Buddy had to stop the block while Nick fished the ring from the pile.

A few hundred fish came over the rail with the last of the net. Buddy gave a disgusted shake of his head, cut the skiff loose, and climbed back to the flying bridge. Nick stood by the rail trying to get his breath back while George and Pete hooked the skiff to the stern and winched it taut. Sweat ran down the inside of Nick's raingear. He felt like he had just played an extra-inning game, but he ran forward to help the other deckhands throw the fish in the hold.

"Alligators," George said. "Cannery ain't gonna want these ugly motherfuckers."

The chum salmon on deck had blackened bellies. Red and green streaks marked their sides and sharp teeth bristled from distorted lower jaws. Some females were so close to spawning that eggs dripped like waxy orange pearls from their vents.

The *Lily* cruised slowly north, Buddy on the flying bridge scanning the water. They passed Cosmos Cove where a few boats were taking turns. Buddy kept going to the next point and once again they set the net.

Danny sat in the *Viking Hero's* skiff while they waited in a line of four boats by Cosmos Cove. Aaron came out of the wheelhouse and lit a cigarette. In Petersburg, Danny had watched from a distance as Aaron sold a baggie to some kid from the beach crew, breaking all their rules. Danny had told him that Mano would be here in two weeks on a processing barge. Mano could sell to all the barge workers and to the boats delivering fish. They would be far away from the cops in town, and Mano would bear most of the risk.

Aaron saw no reason to wait, and Danny was having trouble keeping him in check. In truth, Danny was not all that eager to give Mano a seat at the table. One psychotic asshole was more than enough. He wished he could give Mano and Aaron a knife each and stick them in a cage. With luck, neither one would come out.

A burst of smoke came from the *Hero's* stack. Sven left the lineup and headed for a boat that had set her gear on the point north of them. As they drew near, Danny saw that it was the *Lily Langtry*. She was painted black and gray, like all the old Wrangell creek robbers, and had beautiful, clean lines—the old style, with an open fly-ing bridge, spacious wheelhouse, and the fo'c'sle below decks. Danny had heard that Buddy Stepovich was running the *Lily* this year. Back when Danny started fishing, Buddy had been a high-line skipper, but he had been gone a long time. Fallen into the bottle, the story was.

The *Lily*'s net came aboard. The *Viking Hero* ranged up alongside and backed down hard. Sven came out of the wheelhouse, his big face red as a ham.

"What the fuck you think you're doing, cutting us off," he yelled at Buddy, who ignored him.

Uh-oh, Danny thought and tried to shrink into his raingear. The *Lily* had not set that close to them, and there weren't enough fish to make a fuss over anyway. The *Lily*'s skiff man flipped them the bird. One of the James boys from Craig, Danny thought.

"You been gone too long, old man," Sven shouted. "You don't belong up here no more."

Like the tar baby, Buddy just kept on sayin' nothing.

"Just stay the hell out of my way." Sven went back in the wheelhouse, slamming the door. The *Viking Hero* turned back south. Danny shook his head. What was Sven's problem? Back in the day, Buddy's dad, Milo, had been the man everybody watched; the skipper who always made the right move, always caught the most fish. Buddy had been the heir apparent till he disappeared. Maybe Sven was trying to stake his own claim to being The Man. As if anybody gave a fuck.

Danny looked back over his shoulder. The *Lily Langtry*, not intim-idated, was setting her net again. Good for Buddy.

After the next set, Buddy motioned for Marcus to come aboard, then headed east across Chatham Strait. Marcus came forward with the skiff's safety line and made it fast to a cleat on the deck winch.

"What's up?" Nick asked him.

"Must be gonna try the Admiralty shore."

"What was that scene with the *Viking Hero* all about?"

"Just Sven bein' an asshole." Marcus stripped off his raingear. "It's gonna take about an hour to get across. How 'bout some lunch?"

In the galley Pete sat at the table, sound asleep with his mouth open. George already had the cribbage board and a deck of cards out, waiting for Marcus. Nick wanted to sit down and rest, but he had talked his way into the job by volunteering to cook. He put a frying pan on the stove and began to make burgers.

Marcus shuffled the cards. "I heard this story," he said, "where they had a retirement party for the PFI cannery manager a couple years ago, and Sven picked a fight with the guy. Gave him a bloody nose. At his retirement party."

"Somebody oughta cut him a new asshole," George said. "Him and his skiff man both, the shit they pull."

"They catch fish, though." Marcus dealt the cards.

The three at the table were brothers or cousins, Nick wasn't sure. Tlingits from an outer coast village. Marcus had told Nick that he would be leaving after one or two more openings. He usually worked on another boat and was just waiting for that skipper to come back from the Bristol Bay fishery in western Alaska. Nick figured that when Marcus left, the other two were sure to follow.

Nick put the burgers and condiments on the table and took a plate up to Buddy on the flying bridge. Buddy sat hunched behind the big steering wheel, wearing a heavy jacket over his rain pants, a cloth cap pulled low over his eyes.

"You want coffee?" Nick asked. Without a word, Buddy handed Nick his cup, a big insulated mug with the logo of a Seattle ship chandlery.

When Nick returned with the coffee Buddy threw his half-eaten hamburger over the side and fished a small Three Musketeers bar from his pocket and popped it in his mouth. Nick lingered on the bridge. He wanted to ask Buddy if he was doing okay on deck. A cardinal sin—asking the boss for a compliment. Nick would never make the mistake in a normal job, but fishing was different. He was so far out of his own element that he wanted someone to tell him that at least he was not in the way.

"Where are we going?" he asked instead, then wondered if that might also be an inappropriate question for a skipper.

"Chaik Bay," Buddy said and pointed ahead. "Tides are small enough we can fish the outfall there."

"What do the tides have to do with it?"

"Everything." Buddy grinned. "Ebb comes across the reef there like a waterfall. Fish it on the big tides, it'll take your net, then your skiff, maybe even your boat."

"Oh," Nick said. He knew he had a lot to learn. He picked up Buddy's empty plate and went below. So far Buddy seemed like an okay boss and maybe even a potential friend. When Marcus gave Nick his chalk talk, Buddy had caught Nick's eye and given him a wink and a grin. They were about the same age and Nick could tell they shared a lifelong struggle with alcohol, a battle that created an unspoken understanding.

In the galley, Pete shook an empty ketchup bottle over his second burger. "You got any more ketchup?" he asked Nick.

"Sorry, that's it." When Nick came aboard two days ago there had been three full bottles in the cupboard. Where had it all gone? Pete held the empty bottle up against the light and studied it with a disappointed frown.

They made two sets at Chaik Bay and then finished the day farther south at Point Gardner. Nick began to learn the rhythm of the work. He was still totally confused about the overall process, but with each set, the lead line became easier to stack. The work was not as hard as pouring concrete or baling hay, but the tension of dealing with the unfamiliar was exhausting.

The sun was low in the west when Buddy finally called it quits. The deck crew lifted the skiff aboard the *Lily* with the big double block, dragging it up and over the stern rail. At the peak of its arc the bow of the skiff swung side to side, menacing as a truculent grizzly, until Marcus slackened the line around the deck winch and gently lowered the skiff onto the net pile.

"How much does this thing weigh, anyhow?" Nick asked as he and Marcus secured the skiff with chain binders.

"The skiff? About the same as a pickup."

"And cost?"

"I got a friend just bought a new one for forty grand."

"Jesus." Nick shook his head. "Where I come from, a skiff is a leaky rowboat with like maybe a cane pole and a bucket of crickets for blue-gill bait."

Marcus only looked puzzled, the description as incomprehensible to him as this new world was to Nick.

Nick stripped off his raingear and headed for the galley. Exhausted though he was, he still needed to cook supper. On the galley table, the empty ketchup bottle caught the low sun and winked at him malevolently as the boat rolled.

CHAPTER 6

The currents enter Wrangell Narrows from
both ends on the flood and meet a little S
of Green Point. . . . During spring and tropic
tides, velocities of 6 to 7 knots may occur.

—US Coast Pilot

The *Lily Langtry* came alongside the unloading dock. Nora could see her name and home port of Wrangell painted on her stern. No wonder the graceful lines had looked familiar. When she was a girl, the *Lily* had been the best boat in Southeast Alaska. Milo Stepovich had owned her, a short man who wore his arrogance like a favorite hat. Who was running her now? A lean, dark man was at the wheel and two Natives held the bow and stern mooring lines.

Midway through the unloading, Nora turned to toss a dark chum in the totes and saw Nick standing close by. Same three-day stubble, same wry grin, but now he was wearing rain pants and a torn halibut jacket like any fisherman.

"These are the ugliest fish I ever saw," she said to him. "You responsible for this?"

"I was just along for the ride." Nick came over and stood beside her, his head level with her waist as she stood on the raised catwalk of the sorting table. Nora was suddenly conscious of how dowdy she must look in a slime spattered apron and red bandanna. She resisted the temptation to reach up and touch her hair.

"So you found a job," she said. "Lucky you."

"Deckhand and cook."

"Cook?"

"Hey, nobody's died yet."

Nora shook her head. "So who's your skipper?"

Nick nodded toward the tally shack where the saturnine man

leaned, smoking a cigarette and watching the scales. "Buddy Stepovich."

"Oh, yeah, he's a good fisherman, you're lucky."

Nora picked up another chum—misshapen, discolored, bones sticking through the flesh. She threw it on the reject pile. Buddy Stepovich, could it really be? She looked again at the man by the scales. Stubble of gray whiskers, sunken cheeks, corded neck. When she was in grade school Buddy had been the best-looking boy in Wrangell High School. Nora remembered sitting in the bleachers at a basketball game when Buddy slouched in wearing a suede jacket, Italian shoes, a pack of Marlboros in his pocket. The other sixth-grade girls had giggled like it was an Elvis sighting. Buddy's father was Serbian, short and stocky. His mother, Celeste, was Italian and from her, Buddy had inherited glossy black hair and an almost girlish prettiness. Buddy had started running a seine boat when he was only eighteen. He had dropped out of school his senior year—why sit in civics class when you already make more money than the teacher?

Buddy walked over and said something to Nick. Nora turned away, hoping Buddy would not recognize her. What had happened to him in the intervening years? He looked like the tattered remnants of trawl gear found on the outer beaches, snarled and frayed and packed with sand.

Noon the next day, Nick opened the *Guinevere's* windows and lit the oil stove to drive away the damp. He put the kettle on to boil and sat in the captain's chair. The next seine opening was two days away, and the *Lily* would not leave port till the following morning.

Nick was happy to have found a job, but he felt melancholy. He sniffed the musty air and thought of his boyhood home on the outskirts of Detroit. His parents were Hungarian immigrants, and their kitchen always smelled of paprika and smoked sausage and his mother's langos frying in the pan. Then his mother died when Nick was only eleven and the house began to smell of tobacco and whiskey, of burnt food and clothes unwashed in the hamper. His father, Laszlo, had been a lawyer in Budapest, but in America he worked on the assembly line in the Ford River Rouge plant. He died of a heart attack during Nick's second year in the minor leagues, when Nick's star was still on the rise. At least Lazlo had not witnessed his son's fall from grace; Nick was all alone when he hurt his shoulder and went one for forty-one. He had been leading the league in hits and rbi's when it happened. How could a dream go away so quickly?

"Hey, Nick, you're burning daylight." When he heard the shout from the dock Nick went out on deck. Nora was climbing over the rail.

"Only a couple of tenders to unload this morning, so they let us go early. I thought I'd come say hello." Nora looked at the beat-up boats moored nearby. "Nice neighborhood," she said.

"Trailer trash trollers," Nick said. "Thing is, I swear I've seen some of these boats in the old Shamrock Bar and Grill. In a corner booth around closing time, drinking peppermint schnapps. Puddles of water where they dragged their mooring lines across the floor."

Nora laughed but could not help wonder, if she ever got past Nick's wisecracks, would she find anything of value? With her ex-husband, Buck, beneath the macho posturing, there was absolutely nothing. Not one damned thing.

She sat on the rail. Not far away the redheaded kid, Sara Quan's erstwhile friend, worked his way down the dock, stopping briefly at each of the fishing boats.

"You know that kid?" she asked Nick

"I've seen him making the rounds. Makes me feel guilty, just stumbling into a job while he's pounding the docks."

The kid stopped beside them and scanned the *Guinevere's* trolling rig. "Need a deckhand, cap?" he asked.

"Afraid we're dead in the water. Buy you a cup of coffee, though."

"I'd appreciate it," the kid said, grateful for anything other than a curt dismissal. Nick went into the galley and returned with the pot and three mugs.

"Yeah, you feel like an idiot going to the same boats over and over." The kid was sitting alongside Nora now. "Like you're hoping maybe somebody fell overboard in the night. My name's Toby MacGregor, by the way."

"Nick Zoltan," Nick said as he handed Toby a mug. "And this is Nora."

"Tyler," Nora said quickly, to disabuse the kid of any notion that she and Nick were a couple, but the kid made the association anyway.

"Nick and Nora," he said, "like *The Thin Man*."

"What's that?"

"A book and then a black-and-white movie, Dick Powell and Myrna Loy?"

"Never heard of it," Nora said, though in truth, she had watched it more than once on one of the old movie channels. So, MacGregor was the kid's name, like Rob Roy.

Nick was not thinking of the movies nor the highlands. "My first baseball glove was a MacGregor," he said musingly. "It was completely shapeless, flat as a pancake. Like I was playing in the Shrove Tuesday league, you know? When I got a little older I spent my paper route money on a nice Rawlings with a deep pocket. Only then I visited Cooperstown and saw Ty Cobb's old glove, and it was flat as a flounder, and I wondered if maybe I'd made a mistake."

"Hey, look, you two want to come to dinner? I was gonna make lasagna." Nora wanted to know what the Shrove Tuesday league was, if it was anything at all, but knew better than to ask.

"Gee, sure, ma'am, if it's not too much trouble," Toby swallowed reflexively, a lone wolf hearing of fat sheep in the fold.

"What's the catch?" Nick grinned at Nora, his eyes crinkling at the corners.

"You gotta mow my lawn. And rake it."

"You got a lawn? Pretty upscale," Nick said.

"It's a basement apartment my cousin found. The house is for sale, and I get a break on the rent for doing the yard work."

Together they headed toward town. As they reached the corner of Main Street, Sara Quan passed by, walking with Rick, one of the cannery foremen. Rick was about twenty-five, already balding and carrying a bit of a belly, but his job enabled him to broker favors. Which explained Sara's presence, Nora thought. Sara wore tight shorts and a T-shirt that showed her midriff. Around her navel there was a tattoo of a crescent moon and three stars. Nora tried to remember if her own belly had ever been that flat. Probably not.

Sara did not look their way, but as she passed, she put something extra into the sway of her hips. Nora could feel Toby tense up beside her.

"The beach crew on parade," Nora said in a soft voice. "Toby, didn't I see you with Sara the first day she came to work?"

Toby blushed so hard his freckles looked pale. "Yeah, we came up together. She was sort of my girlfriend. Was."

"At Stanford?" Nora remembered Sara's sweatshirt.

"That's Sara. I just started grad school at Berkeley."

"But now you want to be a fisherman?"

"Sara's idea. She had a friend who made big money up here. Plus, it sounded like an adventure. But after a week in tent city, she moved out. Somehow the rain was all my fault."

"It probably was. What are you studying, computers and stuff?"

"Sara is. Math/physics is her line. Me, I'm an English major."

"Opted for the big bucks," Nick said.

"Yeah, right," Toby said ruefully. "Maybe it's genetic. My dad teaches literature at the University of Michigan."

"Ann Arbor, no kidding?" Nick said. "I'm from Detroit—Allen Park." They bumped fists.

Geographical bonding, Nora thought, as well as the brotherhood of baseball. She felt outnumbered, but they were in Alaska now, her home turf.

Nora's rental had once belonged to Sven Oslund, the *Viking Hero*'s skipper. Now his ex-wife had it up for sale. The grass on the lawn was long, the dandelions blowsy. Nora had been too tired at night to keep up her end of the yard work bargain. Toby wheeled an old hand mower out of the garage while Nick searched for a rake.

Nora started a pot of water for pasta and began to chop onions. Through the open window she could hear the snick-snick of whirling mower blades, an almost forgotten sound.

Nora assembled the lasagna and stuck it in the oven. She poured a glass of wine, went outside, and sat on the stoop. The lawn was already cut and neatly raked. Nick and Toby were playing basketball now, slap of the ball on the concrete driveway, rattle of the rim above the garage door. Toby was at least three inches taller than Nick but gangly rather than smooth. Nick was a better shooter but unwilling to jump—the legacy of middle age. He backed Toby in toward the basket but missed a hook shot. Toby went up for the rebound, but Nick gave him an elbow in the ribs and got the ball back. They both laughed, and Nora felt a flash of irritability at the domesticity of the scene, the boys playing ball while supper cooked. It was a fantasy of family life she no longer trusted, like reaching for one of those chocolates with caramel centers that end up stuck to your teeth. Her own reality was sorting fish in the rain with no idea what winter would bring.

Toby's next shot clanked off the rim. Nick made a halfhearted stab, but the ball bounced down the driveway. A man walking by grabbed it. Nora saw it was Buddy Stepovich.

"Oh, captain, my captain," Nick shouted.

Buddy walked partway up the driveway and launched a clumsy two-handed set shot that started at his waist. The ball kissed the backboard and went through the hoop. Buddy had to be more surprised than any of them, but he acted as though it happened every time.

"Nora and Toby," Nick said as Buddy drew closer. "This is my skipper, Buddy Stepovich."

"We've met," Nora said as Buddy and Toby shook hands.

Buddy looked at her. Up close he appeared even more ravaged. His irises were oddly colored, brown but with a pattern of flecks like shattered quicksilver. His teeth were yellow and worn. His eyes suddenly lit with recognition. "Nora Johnson, right?" he said. "You were Fourth of July Queen in Wrangell one year and then married Buck Tyler?"

"Unfortunately," Nora said about both experiences.

"Where's Buck these days?"

"Drowned."

Buddy nodded as though, like the set shot, it was no more than he had expected.

"Where you been, skip?" Nick asked.

"I thought there was an AA meeting at the church, but nobody was there."

"Well, come on in," Nora said. "I was just gonna put supper on the table. Has to be better than an AA meeting."

Nick and Toby stayed outside to bag the grass clippings. Buddy watched Nora make a salad. "I heard your dad died," Buddy said.

"Almost five years now. And mom died the year after."

"Sorry, I've been kind of out of touch with Wrangell."

"They'd actually been in Sequim since Dad retired. How about your folks?"

"Mom's fine, but Milo had a stroke last winter. Has to use a walker now but he's noisy as ever."

"That's why you're running the *Lily*?"

"Yeah, I've been out of fishing a long time. Don't even have a permit, I'm using the old man's on a medical transfer."

There was little table talk during dinner, no sounds other than the clash of cutlery and the sound of forks scraping empty plates. Nora took it as a compliment but still there was a sense of misplaced effort, with all her work disappearing so quickly, nothing left but dirty dishes.

Buddy pushed his plate back. "Now why can't you cook like that?" he asked Nick.

"This next trip I'm gonna hook up a ketchup bottle with an IV drip at each bunk, so they can mainline the stuff. Maybe two bottles for Marcus."

"Marcus is gone," Buddy said. "He flew back to Craig this afternoon."

"That was kind of sudden."

"Yeah," Buddy said. "I was hoping to get one more trip out of him. Now I gotta put George in the skiff, pick somebody else off the docks."

"Here's your man right here." Nick knew he was being way too familiar with his boss, but he figured somebody had to go to bat for Toby.

Buddy looked at Toby. "You ever been on a fish boat?"

"Nope, never." Toby didn't even try to dissemble.

"Hey, is that really necessary?" Nick asked.

Buddy looked at Nick and grinned. "Apparently not. Yeah, sure, Toby, bring your gear aboard. I won't find anybody experienced this late." He took a drink from his glass of water. "Fish and Game gave us two days out west, and the weather's gonna be bad."

"Baptism of fire," Nick said.

Later Nora stood at the kitchen sink doing dishes. Left behind as usual. She looked out at the long shadows of evening and saw two people walking up the sidewalk to the house's main entry. A little late for prospective buyers, Nora thought. Craning her neck, she could see that it was Sven Oslund and the cook from the *Viking Hero*. She heard the door open overhead; the realtor must not have changed the locks. Muted voices and low laughter echoed in the empty house. Could previous renters hear this well, or was it a characteristic of empty houses?

What was Sven doing here? Cousin Steve had told her it was an ugly divorce. The previous renter had been a young guy, a teacher at the high school, and Sven's wife, Dora, had run off with him, a year ago now. Big Petersburg scandal. "So Sven fishes herring, black cod, salmon, right?" Nora had said to Steve. "He's gone eight, nine months of the year, but expects the little wife to just stay put and keep the house tidy? Plus he's boffing the cook or some barmaid every chance he gets. I say good for Dora."

Voices murmured above, from the master bedroom Nora thought. Sven might be seeking some weird sort of revenge. Or maybe the bed was just bigger than the captain's berth and cheaper than a motel; Nora could never understand men's motives.

There was a brazen burst of laughter and then the sharp crack of a slap. A scream strident as a jay, and then "Fuck you," in a shrill taunt.

Nora heard the quick tap of heels the length of the house. The front door slammed and through her window she could see the woman hurrying down the street, head bowed. Overhead, the crash of something thrown against a wall and then silence.

Fifteen minutes later Nora brewed a last cup of tea and watched the swirls of the infusion. She heard the quiet click of the front door lock. Sven left the house, broad shouldered against the waning light.

CHAPTER 7

Calder Rocks are dangerous kelp-marked
reefs off the E shore of Sumner Strait . . .
a lighted buoy is close W of the N end.

—US Coast Pilot

The *Lily's* bulwark splintered as the skiff slammed into it. George fought the wheel, a stricken look on his face. A big sou'wester had blown in. It was a good fishing wind for Noyes Island, pushing the salmon right on the beach, but it overlaid a pattern of northwest swells, making the surface choppy. Jackass seas, Buddy called them, with no rhythm or pattern.

Things were not going well on the *Lily*; George was having trouble in the skiff and there was chaos on deck. Pete seemed a little confused when giving orders but luckily Toby figured things out quickly. After three sets, he was virtually the deck boss, even though he periodically leaned over the rail and puked. Nick was seasick himself and more than willing to let Toby take charge.

The second day, the seine caught on a snag, and they had to haul it back over the stern, then duck into Little Roller Bay to mend the rip. Buddy blamed no one, but George made so many voluble excuses that Nick figured somehow it must have been the skiff man's fault. Then in the late afternoon, George lost it completely and started screaming at Buddy. Rather than argue, Buddy called it quits for the opener. They picked up the skiff and started the all-night run to town.

Danny Sullivan came on watch at Calder Rocks just before first light. *Vargtimmen*, the old Norwegian fishermen called it, the hour of the wolf. The time when most people are born and most die.

Rays of sunlight broke through the clouds; the storm was gone.

Danny stretched and grimaced at the shooting pain in his back that came from two hard days in the skiff. He needed more ibuprofen, maybe four pills this time, with a cup of coffee to wash them down.

On his way to the galley, he looked toward the fo'c'sle. Melody's bunk was empty. Danny shook his head in disbelief. During the opening, Melody had been near collapse, seasick and over-amped on pills. Danny was sure this would be her last trip on the *Hero*. Either she would quit or Sven would fire her. If Melody was still willing to share Sven's bunk, she was a glutton for punishment. Or at least one of them was.

As he poured his coffee, he heard the stateroom door open. He looked up, half expecting to see Melody, but Sven walked by, mumbling something. Through the doorway, Danny saw him lean over the rail to piss, one hand on the rigging. Danny headed back toward the bridge, but the stateroom door was banging to the ship's roll, Sven having neglected to close it. Danny detoured slightly to latch the door and almost inadvertently looked at the bunk. It was empty. With a faint premonition of trouble, he went to the head and tapped gently on the door. There was no answer and he opened the door and looked inside. Nothing.

Sven came back inside pulling up his sweatpants and scratching his belly.

"Where's Melody?" Danny asked.

"The fuck should I care?"

"She's not in her bunk."

Sven walked to the fo'c'sle and stood staring at the bunk, still scratching his belly absentmindedly. He took another step forward and looked closely at the two sleeping deckhands, as if checking to see if Melody was sharing a bunk, which had not occurred to Danny. Then Sven pulled open the door to the head without knocking.

"Son of a bitch," he said and turned and growled at Danny, "Get back on the wheel."

Danny headed back to the bridge. He heard the roar of the diesel as Sven opened the engine room door and started down the ladder. The last place Melody would ever be, but also the last place left to look.

Once topside, Danny looked at the back deck and the power skiff chained on top of the seine pile. Not a sign of life. The *Hero's* wake stretched south. Most of the fleet had left the fishing grounds early, but there were two seine boats a couple miles back. If they had seen anything they would have called.

Sven appeared, scowling. "You didn't hear nothing?" Danny shook his head. "Motherfucker," Sven said and reached over and put the throttle in neutral. As the boat coasted, he checked the GPS and noted their position in the log. Putting the wheel over, he turned the boat 180 degrees and headed back at a low rpm.

"Keep an eye out," he told Danny and reached for the VHF. "United States Coast Guard, this is F/V *Viking Hero*, WSV 4583."

"This is the United States Coast Guard, Juneau Alaska Group, back to the caller."

"Yeah, this is the fishing vessel *Viking Hero* inbound in Sumner Strait. Looks like we lost a man overboard in the night. We're turning back to search and would appreciate help from any vessels in the area."

"*Viking Hero*, what is your exact position?" the Coast Guard voice asked.

"Six miles northeast of Calder Rocks, steering 190 south-south-west."

"And how many are on board your vessel?"

"Here, you talk to the silly bastards," Sven said impatiently and handed Danny the mike. The Coast Guard wanted to know the make and registry of the *Viking Hero*, the number of crew, the amount of safety gear onboard, and whether there were any other vessels in the area. Danny answered the litany of questions while Sven leaned out the window, scanning the water.

The Coast Guard began to talk with nearby boats. "Why don't they just send a goddamn helicopter?" Sven said.

Danny looked at the instrument panel. The sea water temperature was fifty-one, not that cold, but how long could someone last—twenty minutes? Less, if you were seasick and exhausted. And Sven knew it.

"Fuck, fuck, fuck," Sven yelled suddenly and kicked the console so hard that the plywood paneling cracked in a star-shaped pattern. "Fuckin' insurance, fuckin' paperwork, fuckin' every damn thing."

Aaron appeared suddenly, sticking his head above the companionway. "What's up?" he asked.

"Melody's gone overboard," Danny said.

"Stupid bitch." Aaron yawned.

The cannery heard via single sideband radio, and word spread quickly that someone had been lost. Misinformation flowed among the workers, but when the wilder rumors dissipated with the morning fog, they knew that one of the *Viking Hero's* crewmen was gone.

When the beach crew broke for lunch, Nora saw Nick Zoltan staring at the chalk board that listed the unloading sequence.

"You hear the news?" she asked.

"Pretty awful. We listened on the radio, but we were too far ahead to turn back."

"Who was it?"

"The cook. You remember, that blonde-haired woman."

"Jesus God. What happened?"

"Nobody seems to know. Not even where or when. Just somewhere between Timbered Isles and Calder Rocks. I guess she'd been sick the whole opening."

"Jesus God," Nora said again, thinking of the cold water, the darkness, the terror of treading water while the stern of the boat slowly pulled away. Then she remembered the quick tap of heels in the room overhead and the brief glimpse of the woman's back as she hurried away. Gone forever now.

"How'd it go other than that?" she asked.

"Not so good. Really rough, not many fish. It was a long two days."

"How about Toby?" To her surprise, Nora felt a flash of motherly apprehension.

"He did great. Better than me. It was George who couldn't handle life in the skiff. In fact, he quit. He and Pete took their gear off the boat as soon as we got to town."

"Oh, brother."

"So now I'm like senior crewman."

The *Viking Hero* unloaded at 10:00 p.m. Two other boats had come in late, the ones that had helped in the search, but the *Hero* had been further delayed by the need to talk with both the Coast Guard and the state police. The sun was down and a cold wind blew across the docks when the *Hero* finally came alongside the pumps. Nora was reeling from exhaustion after sixteen straight hours of sorting fish.

As the first of the fish slammed onto the sorting table, she saw the *Hero*'s bearded skiff man climb the ladder to the dock, carrying his sea bag. He hoisted the bag on one shoulder and walked off, casting a long shadow in the glare of the mercury lamps.

Next day the gillnet fishing period closed. The first of the fleet reached town around noon, but when the beach crew assembled at the cannery, Sara Quan was not among them. Another young girl manned the scales, a heavyset blonde girl with a sallow complexion. At coffee break, Nora heard that Sara had taken the cook's job on the *Viking Hero*. The prevailing opinion of the beach crew seemed to be envy, because boat jobs paid so much better. A few expressed reservations, but only about the rough seas and the heavy work. No one seemed to find it strange that Sara would be walking in the steps of a dead woman.

Listening to the hum of conversation, Nora felt a tremor of nausea at the idea of sleeping in Melody's bunk, the mattress still bearing the imprint of her body. Maybe the young could be cold-blooded because they believed nothing bad would ever happen to them. They were as incapable of imagining Melody's death as they were of understanding her life. Again, Nora pictured Melody brushing her hair on the back deck, saw again the fading black eye, heard again the shrill laughter in the empty house. Like looking in a mirror.

Late that evening a knock at the door surprised Nora. It was Buddy Stepovich.

"May I come in for a minute?" he asked, cap in hand. He sat at the kitchen table and accepted a cup of tea, to which he added two tea-spoons of honey.

"How'd it go out there?" Nora asked.

"Could've been worse. We got a few sockeye, and the pinks are start-ing to show up."

"Nick and Toby do okay?"

"Great, just great. Nick's easy to be around and Toby, he's a fuckin' natural . . . Oh, sorry, Nora."

Nora made a dismissive gesture. She'd heard bad language before, as Buddy well knew, but he sat silent and almost flustered. After a moment he said, "Thing is, George and Pete both quit."

"I heard. You're not gonna put Nick in the skiff?"

"No," Buddy laughed. "Toby'd be better. But we caught a bit of luck. Danny Sullivan's going to work for us."

"Danny Sullivan?"

"The skiff man on the *Viking Hero*."

"So that's Danny Sullivan. I remember the name from the old days but I can't say I recognized him."

"He's been around forever. Worked for my dad a few times."

"Why did he quit Sven?"

"I dunno. Danny, he's the best skiff man in Southeast Alaska, only he never makes it through the season on one boat. Something always happens."

"Something?" Nora hoped that was not always a deckhand over-board.

Buddy cleared his throat. "But that still leaves us a man short. I'm wonderin' if maybe you wouldn't want to cook for us."

"Tired of Nick's goulash?"

"A little. Mostly I need somebody who's been around boats. I know I can trust you not to get in trouble."

Nora hesitated. She had been around boats, sure, but being a cook also meant working on deck, and she had never stacked gear on a seine boat before. Then she thought of Sara Quan on the *Viking Hero* and her jaw tightened. "I'll do it," she said.

"We don't haul as fast as some boats. I'll take it easy on you."

"You won't have to."

Buddy rose to go. At the door Nora said, "I gotta ask, I always wanted to know why Milo named the boat *Lily Langtry*."

Buddy grinned and Nora saw a trace of the old ladykiller style. "When Dad had her built he wanted the best boat in Southeast. He kept thinking of changes he wanted. The builder was this Englishman in Seattle named Frank Prothero, and he kept grumbling about 'Lily Langtry's bleedin' yacht.'"

"But who was she?"

"Some actress around the turn of the century, sort of like Marilyn Monroe. The kind always dressed in diamonds and furs. So in England sailors started calling any boat that was over fancy 'Lily Langtry's yacht.' Plus she was the Prince of Wales's mistress, and Milo used to fish off Prince of Wales Island a lot, so bingo."

"I see," Nora said, a little confused by the connection.

"Only Mom expected it to be named after her, and when the old man steams into Wrangell harbor with another woman's name on the brand-new boat, the shit really hit the fan."

Nora remembered the Stepovich household had been volatile, with loud voices and the occasional sound of breaking crockery.

"At least it was a dead woman ten thousand miles away," she said.

"For Mom, that wasn't far enough or dead enough."

CHAPTER 8

Noyes Island, about 2.1 miles NNW of
Baker Island, is mountainous with rugged
steep cliffs along the W. shore.

—US Coast Pilot

Sara Quan sat at the galley table reading a book. It was midafternoon, but everyone was asleep other than the man on the wheel. The dim light and the constant thrum of the diesel gave her an eerie feeling, and she decided to go up to the wheelhouse and look around. She climbed the stairs a little tentatively, not entirely sure if it was off-limits. Billy had the wheel watch, the crewman who thought he looked like a country and western singer, who combed his greasy hair *so* carefully.

Bright lights from the electronics, country music on the tape deck. Through the windows Sara could see they were following in the wake of a boat she recognized from the cannery—the *Muskrat*, a tender with a high, blocky wheelhouse and a low work deck forward.

"Hey, sugar, wanna get me a cup of coffee?" Billy said.

"The name is Sara," Sara said coldly. "Sara Quan." She wanted to tell him to take a flying fuck at a rolling doughnut.

"Well, Mzzz Quan, how 'bout a cup of up?"

Sara hesitated; maybe it was a reasonable request. She knew she was supposed to bring Sven his meals up here while they were fishing. She went down to the galley and brought back coffee in one of those squat-bottomed boat cups.

"Thanks, hon." Billy made sure their fingers touched as he took the cup. Sara wiped her hands on her sweatpants pointedly. She noticed a star-shaped crack in the paneling. What had happened?

Billy hooked one thumb over his belt as if trying to call attention to his crotch. He was wearing a big brass belt buckle that had a coin slot and the words, "Insert Coin, Pull Zipper, Action Starts Instantly, Best Taken Orally."

What a total asshole, Sara thought and turned to go. On the tape deck, Merle Haggard had just turned twenty-one in prison.

Sara was wearing her baggiest sweatpants and an extra-large T-shirt she had stolen from Toby, one that said, "Bay to Breakers." Even so, the men's eyes had tracked her constantly since she came on the boat. Normally she liked that, could use it to her advantage, but on the *Viking Hero* there was no place to get away, which gave her a creepy feeling. The *Hero* was bigger than any pleasure boat she had ever been on but smaller than she expected a workboat to be. It was a bit of a tub—squat, functional, and very noisy.

From the fo'c'sle, she could hear a snore like a bandsaw, audible even above the engine. That had to be Eigil, the new skiff man. New to the *Viking Hero* but way old, maybe forty. He had come aboard trailing a reek of whisky and had taken straight to his bunk.

Sara opened the refrigerator, pulled out a Tupperware container, and popped the lid—old Jell-O salad. She wrinkled her nose and pulled out all the other containers, took them to the back deck, and tossed the contents overboard. She watched the stuff disappear in the curling wake. If that was all that remained of Melody's sojourn on earth, it wasn't much of a legacy.

Sara had found virtually no sign that Melody had ever been on-board the *Viking Hero*. The mattress in her bunk was rolled up and the tiny locker at its head was empty, save for a few bobby pins and a bit of Kleenex blotted with lipstick. There was a small mirror on the locker door, but when Sara looked in it, only her own face looked back.

"In the Bering Sea, some winters the body count just gets out of hand," said Danny. "Guys go overboard in pots, get killed in bar fights, get caught in deck machinery. Boats disappear without a trace. It's a war zone out there."

Nick and Toby looked at Buddy for confirmation. He nodded.

"This is pretty low key compared to the Bering Sea, but even in Southeast every year boats sink, people drown. Fishing's a hard life."

"Can't be any worse than Detroit after dark," Nick said.

"Won't there be some kind of investigation?" Toby asked.

"Yeah, maybe after the season. But Sven did all the right things. Had all the right gear. Basically, it's just a 'shit happens' kind of deal."

Nora was scrubbing down the galley after supper. Shit happens, she thought—what kind of thing was that to say about a woman's death? Elegy for a life gone nowhere. She looked at the four men still seated at the galley table. The three older ones held cigarettes. Not too many years ago Nora had been a chain smoker, but not anymore. She walked to the table, waving her hands to dispel the smoke.

"All right," she said. "No more smoking inside. You need nicotine, go to the back deck."

The deckhands looked at the skipper. Buddy stubbed his cigarette out in an overflowing ashtray. "Cook rules the galley," he said.

Nora went out on deck for a breath of fresh air. The *Lily* was anchored in Little Roller Bay. Two trollers were tucked in close to shore, their masthead lights bright against the darkening sky. Another seiner entered the bay, rounded to, and dropped the hook. Nora could hear the rattle of the anchor chain, loud in the evening stillness. A slight swell broke on the rocks at the entrance of the bay. She had forgotten how beautiful the outer coast could be, but despite the tranquility there were butterflies in her stomach when she thought of the next day's fishing. And she remembered the sense of dread the ocean always inspired, no matter how calm its surface.

Snatches of talk and laughter came from the galley. Nick was telling another baseball story. Didn't they ever tire of sports talk? Nora sat on the rail and leaned against a davit. At least the *Lily* was female, even if she was named after some long-dead British floozy.

Offshore by Shaft Rock the next morning, Sara fought the web that poured over the power block like a river. Try as she might she could not get the netting to pile neatly, but if she stopped to straighten it Sven would almost bury her in web. And if she did not allow Aaron enough slack on the cork line, he would jerk the web from her hands, cursing under his breath. Off to port, she could see Eigil side-towing in the skiff, sitting backward, watching them. It looked peaceful out there, why didn't they let her do that job?

The last of the net came over the block, and Sara unsnapped her rain jacket to cool down. She helped hook up the skiff and then came forward across the net pile, brushing one cheek that burned from a jellyfish strand.

No one had warned her about the horror of lion's mane jellyfish. The seine strained the jellyfish from the sea, and as the net passed over the power block, a stinging slime fell like fiery rain. When they hauled the bunt aboard, the fish died thrashing in a pool of red jelly.

Sara had to admit the lion's mane jellyfish had a malevolent beauty. The ones on deck that were still intact looked like soft Tiffany lamps, brilliant crimson and gold. She watched Billy stomp one flat and kick it through the grated scupper.

Sara pulled off her rain jacket and gloves and looked at her fingers; blisters were already forming. The sea was calm, nonetheless her stomach burned and her head ached from the brilliant sun on the waves. Although fishing had not opened till 6:00 a.m. they had gotten up at three to jockey for position, and the crew had wanted breakfast, even at that ungodly hour. Sara figured that she had already put in a full day of work, and it was not yet 10:00 a.m.

Aaron stood beside her. "What do you think of stacking web?" he asked, with his curious downturned smile.

"It's easier than waitressing."

The *Lily Langtry* waited in a five-boat line. A gentle swell broke against the honeycombed rocks that formed the bight. Some long-ago seine crew had painted the boat name *"Denise Marlene"* on the rocks. On the hill above the painted name a flattopped spruce held an eagle's nest. Toby studied it through binoculars.

"How come we're waiting so long?" Nick asked.

"Buddy's playing for the change of tide," Danny said. "He figures there'll be a slug of fish when the current starts back."

Buddy put the boat in gear and crept a little closer to the mouth of the bight. He was sitting at the wheel on the flying bridge, cloth cap pulled low, back hunched, studying the tides.

Toby lowered the binoculars. "There's an eagle sitting up there, but I can't tell if there are any chicks."

"That nest has been there as long as I've been fishing," Danny said. "Twenty years and more."

"I wonder what the eagle thinks, staring out to sea all that time."

"Its next meal."

"Gotta be more than that." Toby turned the binoculars west toward the *Viking Hero*, looking for the figure in bright blue raingear on the back deck.

Danny followed his gaze and laughed. "One thing, kid. Your girl-friend survives the season, she'll end up making more money than you."

The second day of the opening the sea was glassy calm, though a swell from the southwest lifted the water slightly as though the seafloor was quietly breathing. Near Seagull Bluffs Nora watched a strand of bull kelp drift with the tide. The bulb floated, but the stem disappeared into the depths, its holdfast perhaps still clinging to a bit of rock plucked from the ocean bed. The long fronds trailed on the water like the hair of a drowned woman.

Toby was not thinking of kelp. The *Viking Hero* was holding open not far away, and Toby could see Sara on the back deck talking to Aaron. Toby had instinctively disliked Aaron on sight, and now his hands turned to fists watching Sara stand so close they were almost touching.

Toby had met Sara at a party he and friends had crashed. When she found out he was studying literature, she was quick to tell him it was a waste of time. However, she was taking a lit class to fulfill a distributional requirement. She had talked her way into an upper-level Shakespeare seminar that fit her schedule, but it was not going well. She told Toby that Troilus was a dipshit and Cressida should have sent him to sleep with the fishes. So far that was the only sentence in her term paper.

Toby knew what she was angling for and was not too principled to take advantage. He ended up writing her entire paper. It was an interesting challenge, trying to masquerade as a female math major. An improbable romance started but not an easy one. He no longer harbored any illusions about their future, but the hook was set deep, and Toby knew pulling it out would bring blood.

Fishing closed that evening and they lifted the skiff. Toby stopped for a moment to watch the sun dip below sea level, hoping to see the legendary green flash, but once again it escaped him.

"So why'd you say Sara's gonna make more money than me?" he asked Danny when the sun was gone. "We lifted some pretty good bags."

"How many sets did we make in two days?" Danny asked. He filled two buckets with seawater and detergent and handed a long-handled brush to Toby. Nick was already scrubbing the back of the wheelhouse.

"I don't know. A dozen, maybe?"

"And Sven made probably thirty. Do the math."

"Why? I mean, why the discrepancy?"

"Different styles. Buddy likes to play for the big set. Sven likes to keep the gear in the water. Plus, the *Hero* has bigger hydraulics. And Sven half-purses so he can turn the gear over faster."

"Half-purses?"

"He purses from just one end, the bunt end, while he's hauling the wing end. It loses a few fish, but it's way faster. Only the old-timers full purse anymore. Buddy, he's a bit of a museum piece. I half expect him to tie figure eights every set instead of using Westman swivels."

To Toby this was as impenetrable as deconstructionist jargon. When they finished scrubbing the deck, they rinsed the slime off their raingear and went inside the galley. Danny grabbed three beers from the refrigerator. "Yeah, Sven catches fish," he said. "If your girlfriend survives, she'll be a rich woman. Or at least able to stand a few rounds at the bar."

Nora listened from the kitchen sink while she did the dishes. If that's the case, Daniel, she wanted to ask, what made you jump ship?

Toby went forward to clean up so he could take the first watch. Danny stood in the doorway, taking a long pull at his beer. Nora dried her hands and walked over to him.

"What was Melody like?" she asked.

"I dunno," Danny said uneasily. "Just a broad, I mean, you know, a woman."

"Husband? Kids?"

"Two ex-husbands. No kids."

"Where did Sven find her?"

"Ballard," Danny said. He picked at the label of his beer bottle with a broken thumbnail. "Look, if you wanna know, I got her the job. She was sort of my girlfriend for a while."

"And when she got on board the skipper took over?"

"Long-cocked by the boss man. Old story." Danny drained his beer and tossed the bottle overboard.

CHAPTER 9

Wrangell Narrows extends in a general
N direction for 21 miles. . . . The channel is
narrow and intricate in places, between
dangerous ledges and flats, and the
tidal currents are strong.

—*US Coast Pilot*

Rain falling, the *Lily Langtry* stopped at the south end of the Narrows to pull a crab pot they had set before the opener. There were six Dungeness crabs in the pot. Danny pulled them out and flipped them upside down on the deck. While the *Lily* got back underway he baited the pot, and he and Toby tossed it overboard. Nick righted one crab, which scuttled sideways, confused and dazzled by the soft light of morning. Does a crab feel the rain? Or the dry places between the drops?

Danny grabbed one, avoiding the pincers. He immobilized the legs with one hand and with the other ripped the carapace off with a single, swift motion. Then he tore the crab in half.

"Ouch," Toby said, wincing at the quick brutality.

"If you can't stand the killing, you're in the wrong line of work." Danny ripped another crab in half, then took the empty carapace and winged it like a frisbee out across the water.

Nora watched from the galley door as the carapace skipped twice, cartwheeling, before it filled with water and began to sink. Even in death, crabs could not move in straightforward fashion. She picked up the cleaned crabs, took them inside, and dropped them in the big pot she had boiling on the stove. A thick foam rose to the surface.

She thought again of Melody, rolling around now on the sea bottom, prey to crabs and hagfish and everything else. When she and Buck were longlining, sometimes they would pull a halibut aboard and find that sand fleas had consumed everything but the head and skeleton. Not a gentle place, the ocean floor.

Danny reached past her to grab the coffee pot. "The rails on the *Viking Hero*," Nora said to him, "they've gotta be four feet high. How do you fall over something like that?"

"It was rough. She was sick, tired. You know what it's like out there."

"She was your girlfriend?" Somehow it was hard to picture.

"More of a pal, really. She was tending bar. Getting over a bad relationship, looking for a change, so I got her the job. I don't feel too good about it, you wanna know the truth."

"But—"

"Just give it a rest, Nora. Okay?"

In Scow Bay, a blue heron perched on a three-legged piling. It flew as the *Lily* approached, dropping low to the surface of the water, its neck pulled back in a sinuous curve. Its slate gray wings could have been part of the sky, or the water.

At noon, Nora stood at the end of the Petersburg dock. The *Lily Langtry* had unloaded quickly and tied up in the harbor. Buddy and Danny had engine room work to do, but Nick and Toby had persuaded Nora to climb Petersburg Mountain, across the Narrows.

Nora tapped her foot impatiently. How had she let herself get talked into this when all she wanted was a quiet cup of tea and a long bath? She had managed a quick call to Arizona and caught Trish waiting for a cab to take her to work. Her car was in the body shop because her boyfriend, Duane, had been in a fender bender, coming home late from the bars.

"It was really the other guy's fault, Mom," Trish had said, "but the insurance company doesn't see it that way."

"Has Duane got a job yet so he can pay you back?"

"He's got a couple good leads. Look, Mom, the cab's here, gotta run. Love ya."

Leave him, Nora had wanted to scream to the dead phone. Throw the bum out. What was Trish trying to do, recreate her worthless father?

Nick appeared in a small skiff borrowed from the cannery. "Where's Toby?" Nora asked but then saw him walking down the dock, a pack slung over his back, Sara Quan at his side. Oh, great, Nora thought, the only thing lacking—Sara's charming face.

"I ran into Sara and asked her to come along," Toby said when they reached the skiff. "I hope you don't mind. She made us some lunch."

"Plenty of room," Nick said and helped Sara into the bow seat of the aluminum skiff.

They crossed the Narrows and beached the skiff near the trail-head. Sara was wearing shorts and an unbuttoned blue work shirt over a T-shirt with a mission blue butterfly. Her long black hair was loose. She and Toby quickly outdistanced Nick and Nora as the trail switchbacked through the woods.

Spruce needles underfoot, a split-log footbridge across a tiny stream. Dappled light and silence, except for a peal of laughter from Sara on the trail above them. Nora began to feel more tranquil. In the subdued light, she felt as though she were walking along the sea bottom in a kelp forest illuminated by sunlight sifted through seawater.

They passed a wind-fallen tree, the wood of the standing stump oddly bright among the shades of green. Nora heard the quick chatter of a squirrel and the scutter of its feet on the scaly bark. Nothing else moved.

"Nice to see some color other than green," Sara said. She and Toby had reached the peak, and she was half reclining against a reef of gray rock that had bright orange splashes of lichen. "Kind of a monochromatic forest, I wonder who the designer was."

"God."

"Time for him to find another line of work. He's lost his touch." Sara looked around at the patches of tundra and stunted trees.

Toby sat on a rock ledge, chewing a twig. "What mystifies me most, on the boat I mean, is watching the double block when we lift the skiff. There's like four parts of the line going through the movable part of the block, right? And a fifth coming down to the deck winch."

"We just use the cable from a big winch that's mounted on the mast. A Gearmaster, they call it."

"Whatever. The thing about the double block is, the four lines, or five, all go at different speeds around the pulleys, even though they're all part of the same line."

"That's because they're traveling different distances. Didn't anybody ever tell you about mechanical advantage?"

"Yeah, but it's all the same line, for Christ's sake. It's not possible. You can't have a snake with the tail going faster than the head."

"It's known as science, Tobias. You should look into it. You might find something to your own advantage."

"Fuck science. I'm talking about reality."

Nick and Nora appeared from the forest. Nick stopped to look east toward the mainland; Kates Needle and the Devils Thumb stood out sharply against the skyline, bare granite and patches of snow. Looking down he could see the blue waters of Frederick Sound, speckled with a few ice floes from the LeConte Glacier.

"Thanks for bringing me up here, you guys," Sara said. "It's nice just to breathe fresh air. Every time I burp I taste diesel. Our whole boat stinks of it."

"The *Lily* doesn't smell that way," said Toby from where he slouched against the rock. "More like wood and fish and salt. Real musty."

"Eau de fish boat," said Nick.

"The smell of defeat." Nora knew that scent all too well.

"Nothing like that on the *Hero*," said Sara. "It's got the soul of an automatic can opener."

"Danny calls it the Fucking Zero," said Toby.

"Not to Sven's face, I'll bet." Sara rummaged in the pack. "You want a sandwich?"

Without waiting for an answer she flipped a sandwich to Nick who unwrapped it and took a bite. "Wow," he said, "what's this?"

"Steelhead. I grilled it on the boat last night with a paste made of white miso, garlic, a little brown sugar."

"You fed that crew miso?" Nora could not believe this.

"It didn't go over real big. Those guys, talk about meat and potatoes, sheesh. On the way out, we pulled Sven's crab pot. Nice big king crabs. So I make crab fettuccini, what's to not like? Only I use a ginger sauce and spinach fettuccini. Billy looks at it and he's like, 'Guess it'll make a turd.' Bastard. Then he takes a ketchup bottle and completely douses it."

"Ketchup, nectar of the North," said Nick.

"As a student of etymology I feel obligated to point out that ketchup is a Chinese word," said Toby. "So your ancestors bear ultimate responsibility."

"Not my ancestors, buster." Sara rolled on her back and ate her sandwich lying down, one leg crossed over the other, kicking the air idly.

From where he sat Nick could see well up her shorts, which were brief to begin with. And above the waistband he could see the crescent moon tattoo, beckoning as she moved. He caught Nora frowning at him, blushed, and looked away at the granite face of Kates Needle.

"Does the crew hassle you at all?" Nora asked Sara. Not that she would blame them in this case.

Sara sat up. "Nothing I can't handle. Only sometimes . . . it's like, if I want to tell them anything, I should just type it out and tape it to my butt."

"Do they ever talk about Melody?"

"Not one word. Not ever."

"Doesn't that strike you as strange?"

"Whatever they said would be even stranger. You should hear them badmouth your friend Danny."

"Who's the new skiff man?" Nick asked.

"This real old guy named Eigil Andersen. Relatively inoffensive."

"I knew Eigil way back when." Nora knew he was a couple years younger than she was. "He had a troller called the *Happy Hooker*."

"Typical." Sara jumped up. "Look, you guys, I gotta go. Sven's liable to have kittens if I'm not around when he decides to push off. C'mon, Tobias, I'll race you down."

"What mad pursuit? What struggle to escape?" Toby said, still lolling in place. "What pipes and timbrels? What wild ecstasy?"

"Ecstasy, my ass," Sara said and took off running. Toby leaped up and gave chase.

Nick and Nora followed more sedately, Nick pondering the conjunction of ecstasy and ass. Specifically Sara's. "Were we ever that young?" he asked.

"Not me," Nora said. Below them on the trail she could hear the two youngsters whooping loudly and smiled despite herself. Sara's bubbly conversation had surprised her; at the cannery Sara had always been cool and aloof. But there was an odd, revved-up quality to her laugh that puzzled Nora.

When they reached the skiff the tide was out, and they had to wade, dragging the skiff as they followed a little salt creek that meandered across the tide flats. Looking down, Sara saw a small crab pinwheeling along in the current. She grabbed it and tossed it in the boat. There were others as well, bouncing along the bottom. Toby caught a few, and so did Nick.

"Are these street legal?" Nick asked.

"Maybe barely." Nora could not remember the legal minimum size. Sara picked up another that pinched her. She shrieked and then threw her head back and laughed, standing now knee-deep in the creek, her hair loose. Still laughing she knotted the wet tails of her shirt above her shorts. Jesus, she was beautiful, Nora thought with grudging admiration.

"Gotta be the king valve setting," Buddy said.

"You asking me?" Danny looked at the compressor and chiller of the refrigeration unit that had been added to the already crowded engine room a few years before.

"I can always turn it off manually, but if I forget, the chiller will freeze up and we're screwed." Buddy scratched his bristly cheek, leaving an oily smear.

Danny had no helpful suggestions; he was a skiff man, not an engineer. He looked at the bucket of waste oil and the bucket holding the discarded oil filters—Racors and Lubrifiners from the big Caterpillar engine. "I'm gonna take this stuff up and dump it," he said.

Buddy handed the buckets up the engine room ladder, and Danny carried them carefully through the galley and out on deck. There was a waste oil dumpster near the Harbormaster's office, and he carried the heavy buckets up the ramp, stopping to rest twice. While he was pouring the warm oil into the dumpster, Billy Nichols from the *Viking Hero* walked by. Billy wore a blue denim shirt with pearl button snaps and a baseball cap bearing a large pin that showed a drunken Pink Panther lolling in a martini glass. The caption read "Happiness is a Tight Pussy."

Jesus, Danny thought, where was that goofball when the twentieth century was handed out? No doubt Billy was headed for Kito's Kave on Sing Lee Alley, but Danny doubted the hat would help him score, not even at the Kave.

Danny returned to the *Lily Langtry*, stripped off his coveralls, and stood on deck with a tin of waterless hand cleaner, trying to scrub clean. An old Lund skiff crossed the channel, the mountain climbers returning. Come on, Nick, watch the rips, Danny thought as the skiff swerved erratically. Nick brought it alongside the outermost float, and Toby and Nora climbed out, along with that girl Sara that Toby was sweet on. Nick took the skiff back to the cannery and the other three stood talking. The girl was wearing shorts and a shirt tied in a bow at the waist. She arched her back, laughing, and tugged at her wet shorts. Spectacular stems, Danny thought. Maybe there was something to this jogging bullshit after all.

Buddy appeared alongside him, lighting a cigarette. He looked gloomy, still smeared with grease.

"The thing about engine work," Danny said, "I don't mind it too much so long as I got one more trick to try. It's when you run out of options that you realize you're totally fucked."

"Like all the rest of life," Buddy said as he watched Sara Quan walk toward the *Viking Hero*.

CHAPTER 10

Cape Ulitka, locally known as Snail Point,
is a neck of land that projects about 0.6
mile in a N direction from the NW end of
Noyes Island.

—*US Coast Pilot*

"What is this shit?"

"Daniel," Nora looked up from her own plate of rice and crab salad.

"Hey, no, it's really good, but—cold rice? I've just never had it is all."

"Toby's friend Sara gave me the recipe, but it's Russian, not Asian."

"She can cook too?" Danny asked Toby.

"You oughta try some of her sweet jelly roll," said Toby and Nora rolled her eyes. "Sorry," Toby said. "Old blues tune."

"This boat sure is a learning experience." Danny shook his head. "First boat job I ever had, I'm like fourteen years old, I go gillnetting with this guy named Chester. His boat had an oil stove like this one, and Chester, he'd keep a big roasting pan on it, constantly simmering. He dumped canned goods in it and when he got hungry he'd grab a can and open it. Thing is, all the labels would soak off, so he had no idea what he was getting—corn, peas, chili, those little sweet potatoes, you know? He kept six-packs of Pepsi outside the wheelhouse window. He'd grab a Pepsi, open a can from the stove, that's supper. Or breakfast."

"Oogh," Toby said.

"The boat was a wooden double-ender. Didn't have any plumbing, we just used the deck bucket for a head. I remember one time Chester sitting on the bucket taking a dump, all the while spooning peas out of a tin can."

"Enough, already," Nora said and stood up.

"Hey, I'm only telling a story. It's not like I'm actually doing anything."

Nick laughed. "You can sin by thought, word, deed, or omission."

"That sure doesn't leave much room to maneuver—" Toby started, but Nora missed the rest as she took the remainder of her lunch to the back deck. Comedians. She was adrift with a bunch of would-be comedians. And theologians.

The *Lily* was headed west in Sumner Strait. There was a ten-knot tailwind that made the *Lily* feel motionless, no apparent wind on deck since the air moved at the same speed as the boat.

Back in the galley Nick took a second helping. "Most Stanford girls have tattoos now?" he asked. It was hard to think of Sara and not picture the crescent moon and stars.

"Sara's kind of going through an outlaw phase."

"She'll fit right in on the *Viking Hero*," Danny said. "Only with those guys it ain't a phase. Tell you the truth, kid, she was my girlfriend I'd tell her to get off that boat."

"Think she'd listen?" Nick grinned.

"Sara, she's tougher than she looks. She can hold her own just about anywhere," said Toby.

"She sure had a lot of energy racing up that mountain," said Nick. "I was impressed."

"She was really revved," said Toby. "I hardly recognized her. I don't know what they're putting in her coffee on that boat."

"Excuse me," Danny said and got up from the table. "Time for a smoke."

Through the open door, Toby could see Danny light a cigarette and lean against the rail not far from Nora. Toby looked at Nick, "Was it just me or was there some tension between Nora and Sara yesterday?"

Nick laughed. "That's because, twenty years ago, Nora would have been exactly like Sara. Exactly."

"Do you have any idea why Buddy was away from fishing so long?" Nora asked Danny.

"I heard he was hitting the sauce pretty hard."

"But fifteen years, what was he doing in Seattle?"

"No idea." Danny shrugged. Nora asked way too many questions, but at least she was off the Melody subject. "One time I heard he was working nights as a janitor, cleaning those big high-rises in downtown Seattle."

"Buddy?" Nora could not picture Buddy Stepovich sweeping up computer printouts and empty latte cups from some yuppie scum. Like Samson chained in the temple. "Why would he walk away from something he was so good at?"

"I dunno. Maybe he was too good too young. Plus he lost a boat, the *Mary Eileen*."

"You fish long enough you're gonna sink a boat. Milo lost a couple, didn't he?"

"Yeah, two that I know of. But, thing is, a crewman drowned when the *Mary Eileen* went down. Some kid from Kake. He got trapped in the fo'c'sle when the boat rolled over. They could hear him knocking on the hull but couldn't get to him. And then she sank. I'll bet Buddy heard that knocking for a long time."

Noon on the first day of the opener, Sara looked north along the coast of Noyes Island. Dozens of seine boats worked their gear, nets spilling from the power blocks above the deck. They looked like mechanical spiders, endlessly spinning their webs.

The *Viking Hero* was holding open close inshore by Little Roller Bay, the skiff almost on the beach. When they hauled back, a brittle star and two sea cucumbers were in the bunt along with the salmon. Sara took a filleting knife and began to clean the sea cucumbers, cutting free the long muscles that she knew tasted like tender abalone.

"They call those 'fisherman's cocks,'" Billy said to her. "Stroke 'em and they get hard."

"What's that got to do with fishermen?"

"You really want to know, sugar?"

Sara stuck the tip of her knife in the wooden deck grate and considered orchiectomy as an appropriate response. She looked at the sea cucumber muscles, pink and firm.

"You ain't gonna feed us any of that gook shit?" Billy asked.

"They're for me. For you, chicken fried banana slug."

Later, working in the galley, Sara felt the pressure of someone's gaze. Turning she saw Aaron in the doorway drinking a Coke and staring at her. He was wearing orange rain pants and a black Harley T-shirt. His forearms and biceps were covered with tattoos, swirling reds and greens and blues. Sara locked eyes with him, irritated by the scrutiny and unwilling to waver. After a moment, Aaron crushed the Coke can with one hand and turned away, his eyes sliding off her like the headlights of a car passing at night.

By 4:00 p.m. the second day the *Lily* was fully loaded, fish spilling over the coaming when they shipped the hatch covers. Buddy elected to tow the skiff all the way to Petersburg rather than lift it onto the overloaded boat.

Danny looked over the side. The guards were down to water level, the decks almost awash. He shook his head. "She had such a sweet ride in the old days, they never should've put a tank in her."

"Why did they?"

"Had to. The cannery won't buy from dry boats anymore. You gotta be tanked and refrigerated."

"So you fished on the *Lily* before?" Toby asked.

"A couple of seasons with Milo years ago. Got fired both times. Milo was the best fisherman in Southeast, but what an asshole. He never stopped yelling."

"Doesn't sound like Buddy. When Nick and I screw up, Buddy just shakes his head mournfully, maybe laughs a little."

"Buddy was a hardass as a young skipper, trying to make his mark. But somewhere, somehow, something really changed."

The *Lily* transited Wrangell Narrows in dead-of-night dark; the buoys that marked the channel flashed red and green as though the boat was trapped inside a pinball game. The *Lily* was the first boat to reach the cannery. Nora talked to some of her former coworkers on the beach crew. The gossip was that Eric had flipped out, babbling nonsense, and stripping to his skivvies right on the sorting table. The medic had sedated him and sent him to the hospital. The next day he was medevacked south. Nora wondered how his Seahawks cap had coordinated with a straitjacket.

Buddy came down from the cannery office and walked over to Nora. "When you shop you might want to get enough food for two, three weeks."

"What's up?"

"The cannery's bringing a processing barge down from Bristol Bay. It'll be anchored in Warm Chuck. We'll get dock delivery price there, so we'll just stay on the grounds from now on. If we get a chance we'll slip into Craig for groceries, but no telling when."

"Oh, boy," Nora shook her head. "Time to pay the piper." She knew that life had been too easy, the seas too calm, the fishing too slow. And the food, where was she going to put it all? Locusts had more moderate appetites than her crew.

Nick helped her with the shopping, but then Nora needed to be alone and headed for her apartment. The *Lily* would not be leaving till morning and she did not want to pass up a last chance to listen to silence. Next to the Harbormaster's office there was a bank of pay phones and on impulse she called the Coast Guard office in Juneau. A woman answered the phone and Nora asked her for information on the Melody Kupchak investigation. The woman was unwilling to tell her anything other than that the hearing would be in September at the earliest.

"Will it be open to the public?" Nora asked.

"Do you have pertinent information?" Nora sensed the woman getting out a pencil.

"Not really, I just knew Melody." She hesitated. "Listen, you don't have an address where I could send a sympathy card or something?"

"Next of kin is a sister in Bakersfield." The woman gave Nora the address and then for a moment the official mask slipped. "I had to call the sister about the personal effects. She didn't seem too interested, kind of annoyed, actually."

Nora thanked the woman and rang off. What was she babbling

about, a sympathy card? Might as well scream your pain at the mountains. Or post a letter in Warren Channel.

She took a roundabout route to her apartment to savor being on land—the smell of flowerbeds and the sound of children playing. On Sing Lee Alley, Eigil Andersen stumbled out of Kito's Kave. He stopped and looked at Nora as if a lightbulb had just gone on.

"Nora," he said. "Buck's woman. I heard you was back in town."

"Hey, Eigil." Nora was not happy at the intrusion.

"So how's Buck?"

"Drowned."

"No kidding?"

"The Columbia Bar," Nora said, thinking that, no, she was not, in fact, kidding.

"Oh, yeah, I heard, only I forgot. Sorry."

Nora looked at him. Tall but stooped over, big hands, and muscular forearms. He wore a dirty, pinstriped logger's shirt, blue sweatpants tucked into his socks, and those pull-on shoes they called fisherman's slippers. He had an oft-broken nose, red-rimmed eyes, and big clusters of broken blood veins on his cheeks. He looked as though he had hoed a hard row.

"You're not trolling anymore?" Nora asked.

"Naah, I don't do too good on my own. The hooch, you know. I'm more of a team player. Mostly I been working the draggers."

"How do you like working for Sven?"

"That fuckin' jarhead. He ain't the man I used to know."

"He ever talk about Melody?"

"Who?"

"The cook that went overboard."

"That Chinese girl?" Eigil said with a puzzled expression. "I just seen her."

"Never mind."

They passed the Sons of Norway Hall, a frame building with a gambrel roof, fresh white paint, and shutters painted with floral patterns—rosemaling. Inside a potluck was happening and they heard the hum of voices and the ring of laughter.

"I quit the boat," Eigil said suddenly. "I'm still on probation from that last bar fight, can't be around the dealing." He shook his head ponderously. "No, sir, not Eigil."

"Dealing?" Nora stopped short.

"You know, crankster gangsters." Eigil waved his hand vaguely.

"Is that why Danny quit?"

"Danny?" Eigil snorted. "Danny Sullivan? In Petersburg, Danny Sullivan's always been the man to see, you wanted anything. He's been in the pen once; you'd think that'd be enough."

"Danny never mentioned the dealing."

"The last thing you wanna do is believe a single word that little prick says."

Eigil looked around, then turned to walk back toward the bar as if forgetting he had just come out. He called back, "You see Buck, tell him I said hey."

CHAPTER 11

*Cape Addington is the SW extremity of the narrow
tongue of land which for two miles is less than 0.5
mile wide and forms the SW end of Noyes Island.
The extremity of the cape is a rocky knob, 65 feet
high, cut by deep crevices.*

—US Coast Pilot

"Buddy . . . ," Nora said, then hesitated. "Eigil Andersen told me Danny had been in prison. You know anything about that?"

"I heard about it," Buddy said reluctantly. He and Nora and Toby were sitting in the galley of the *Lily* outbound in Sumner Strait. Buddy took a roll of Life Savers out of his pocket, unwrapped it, and laid three of the candies in a row on the table. He spun them around like a shell game. "Something to do with drugs. All I know is he's the best skiff man I've ever seen. It's a waste he's not running a boat."

Toby looked at the Life Savers, two cherries and a lemon. They looked different, somehow, in the context of a work boat, where life savers were more salt than sweet.

Toby did not mind asking Danny about his record.

"Possession with intent to sell," Danny said. "It was only marijuana, but the judge nailed me to the cross. Wanted to show he was a hard ass."

"How did you get popped?"

"Sold a baggie to this little blue-eyed blonde in a bar. Down in Ballard. I was trying to play the big shot. Shit, she didn't look old enough to be in the bar, let alone a fuckin' narc."

"Isn't that entrapment?"

"Naah. I broke the cardinal rule—never sell to somebody you don't know. I was stuck on stupid, like all the other dumbfucks ended up in Walla Walla."

"What was it like?"

"Doing time? Boring. About like watching the anchor rust. And hot, Jesus! Walla Walla in the summer, you'd stick to your fucking cot with sweat."

"Did you miss fishing?"

"Are you kidding?"

"Well, you know." Toby grinned and waved his arm vaguely. "The romance of the sea and all."

"Romance? It's a fucking marriage."

"But you keep coming back."

"It's all I know."

"Was your dad a fisherman?"

"Fuck no, he was a teacher. The principal of Petersburg High, actually. Plus, my mom was a teacher, and now my older sister. I am most definitely the black sheep."

Toby nodded. Back home he had known a principal's son who went to great lengths to prove he was wilder than anyone.

"I don't know," Danny said. "Growing up in Petersburg, if you weren't Norwegian, you weren't nothin'. Every day in school was a battle. I couldn't wait to get out of that fuckin' place. After my first summer seining, I bought a scooter—an old Harley 74. I dropped out of school and gypsied up and down the West Coast. Thought I was free as a bird. I'd ride up to a beach someplace, rap my pipes to let the babes know I was there, then take my pick. They knew the rules, no butt, no putt."

"Doesn't sound so bad."

Danny laughed, short like a bark. "Yeah, well I thought I got away. Ran away from home but somehow I'm still here. Can't keep from circlin' back."

The next day the wind blew thirty knots southeast, but fishing was good. Each set was a struggle, particularly when the tide began to run back against the swell. At noon, the *Lily* had a big set, one with too many fish in the bunt to lift. Danny brought the skiff alongside and they rigged the brailer, a net bag with a long aluminum handle.

Danny, Nick, and Nora hardened up the web to concentrate the fish, and Toby dipped the big brailer in the bunt. When it was full Buddy lifted the brailer with a line from the deck winch, and Toby swung it across the deck and dropped it in the hold, loosening the thin chain that held the bottom closed. He then swung the brailer back to take another dip. Toby had to fight to keep his footing on the tilting deck, but he was pumped up at the sight of the frenzied fish in the net and yelled like a banshee when the fish dropped in the hold.

They took six dips with the brailer and then put a line around the bunt and winched the remainder of the load aboard. Buddy instantly ran to the flying bridge and kicked the *Lily* in gear without waiting to hook up the skiff. Danny followed, his skiff pushing a big bow wave.

While they brailed, the *Lily* had drifted way back beyond the Haystack, and now she was headed back to the bight at full throttle. There was only one boat waiting in line, but the *Viking Hero* was charging in from the outside with her net still over her block, racing the *Lily* to be next in line.

The two boats converged at almost right angles and reached the bight simultaneously. Buddy throttled back and a moment later the skiff caught up with them. Danny came forward to help clear the deck.

"So who won?" Toby asked him.

"Almost a dead heat, but I think we got there first."

"How do they decide anyway?"

"There's a protocol, but it's kind of uncertain. Whoever gets to the waiting area first. But it depends on where you figure the line is."

When the boat ahead of them set out, both the *Lily* and the *Hero* edged out of the bight. Sven came out of the wheelhouse, his shirt billowing in the wind, and yelled, "It's my set, goddamnit."

Buddy looked at him for a moment, looked at the water, then made a go ahead gesture with one hand and turned the *Lily* back into the sheltered waters of the bight. Danny frowned. "Can't let him do that," he said to Toby. "Can't let him push us around."

They waited another twenty minutes in the bight while the *Hero* held open. But when the *Lily* finally took her turn, the fish were there. They had to take ten dips with the brailer, nearly filling the hold.

"We did better than the *Hero*, didn't we?" Toby asked Danny.

"Way better. We got the change of tide. I don't know if we just got lucky or Buddy was playing the fox, lettin' Sven go first." Danny grinned and rubbed his whiskers. "Our boy is definitely getting his stroke back. I been fishin' a long time, but Buddy, he's got something extra. What he sees and what he knows about this coast . . . Remember last opener when we set in that rip and the seine went totally bug fuck? It collapsed and we got all those fuckin' gillers when we hauled back?"

"Yeah," Toby said slowly.

"The next set Buddy drops me off the same place only he takes off at this weird angle and I'm thinkin', 'What's up, my man?' only when he hits the end of the seine and turns, the rip opens the net up pretty as a picture, a perfect hook."

Toby looked at Nick. Nick just shrugged.

"Fuckin' artistry," Danny shook his head. "Fuckin' genius. Wasted on you lemon farmers."

"Lemon pickers," Nick said as though the distinction was important. "Lemon pickers."

Sara pulled off her rubber gloves and rain jacket and went into the galley. Once inside, she stripped off her rain pants and kicked them in the corner. If the *Hero* stayed in the calmer waters of the bight for twenty minutes she might just be able to get supper in the oven.

The day had been chaotic. When Eigil quit, Sven had hired some high school kid named Scott and told Aaron that he would now be the skiff man. To Sara's surprise Aaron had flat refused, facing Sven down. Which left Billy. Billy claimed to have worked as a skiff man for a season on a Craig boat, but Sven was none too pleased with his performance. When Billy was side-towing, Sven would get so exasperated that he would go to the rail, point angrily in the direction he wanted Billy to tow, and scream curses at the top of his lungs. Even so, the net came in completely misshapen, with lots of gillers, and the web chafing strip rolled around the lead line. Plus, on their third set of the day Billy had caught the skiff towline in the propeller. They had to tow him into shelter, lift the skiff, and free the line, losing fishing time.

At least Billy was no longer in the galley with his mindless chatter. The kid, Scott, sat at the table when they weren't working, endlessly turning the pages of old *Hustler* magazines.

Sara took a pot roast out of the refrigerator and put it in a skillet to sear. As she quartered an onion she felt the boat move slowly out of shelter back into the lumpy seas. Oh, shit, she thought, feeling more than a little harried. She dumped the roast and onion into a pot and opened the refrigerator to look for carrots when the boat took a sudden lurch. She turned to grab the roast and lost control of the door. A carton of milk and a glass container of apple juice flew out and smashed on the galley floor, followed by half a dozen apples.

"Motherfucker," Sara yelled, as she sucked a burnt finger. Scott looked up from his magazine and laughed. Apples rolled across the galley floor through the broken glass and spilled milk and juice. A wave pattern started in the wake of the apples. Sara felt like breaking another bottle on Scott's head. To her surprise, Aaron came into the galley and picked up the apples and then got down on his hands and knees and began to pick up the broken glass and throw it in the wastebasket.

"Thank you," Sara said as she returned to the cooking. "I really, really appreciate that."

"De nada," Aaron said. He mopped the floor and then went on deck to rinse the mop. Sara watched him go, grateful for the first act of kindness shown during her sojourn on the *Viking Hero*.

The main engine growled again as Sven moved out to set the net. Not again, Sara thought. How was she going to make it through the day? She was not at all sure it was a good idea to ask Aaron for more of those little pills; the energy from them felt alien, intrusive—a dance like the tarantella, from the bite of a spider.

The *Lily* had a deck load before quitting time. When she reached Cape Ulitka, there were three tenders at anchor but at least a score of seine boats. Buddy called on the radio and was given an estimated

2:00 a.m. unloading time. The *Lily* dropped the hook near the head of the bay to wait her time. Curtains of rain kited across the crowded anchorage and the sound of diesel engines, deck winches, and fish pumps echoed from the hills. Deck lights and spotlights crisscrossed, outlining the moving hulls in an almost strobe effect.

After supper, Nick lay down in his bunk, fully clothed. Toby fell asleep before he finished eating, head down on the table. Nora carefully cleared the table, trying not to wake him. Danny was on the back deck, smoking a cigarette in the lee of the wheelhouse while he watched the dance of rain in the spotlights. He came back in the galley and got a beer from the refrigerator. Nora looked at him—haggard face and bloodshot eyes, but he was upright and unruffled.

"Don't you ever get tired?" she asked.

"This ain't so bad. It's nothing like longlining in the Gulf, or crabbing out of Dutch. The Bering Sea in winter makes this seem like a cakewalk."

"You and Buddy. It's like nothing ever fazes you."

"You gotta know the rhythm, so you can pace yourself. But, you know, I was just looking around out there, wondering how many years I had left." A spotlight raked the galley windows briefly. Danny leaned against the doorjamb, holding his beer by its long neck. "Hard rain," he said softly.

The *Viking Hero* unloaded to the *Pacific Destiny*, a big crabber moonlighting as a tender. Sara kept tally as each brailer was weighed. The cook on the tender manned the scales; she was an older woman, heavyset and gray haired, wearing a University of Michigan sweatshirt that made Sara think of Toby. Sara noticed a basketball hoop mounted on the *Destiny*'s superstructure. Did they have pick-up games? Three on three in the Bering Sea in twenty-foot seas and forty-knot winds?

Sara ducked back in the galley for a moment's warmth. As the *Hero*'s hold was pumped dry, the boat's trim changed. The bow went slightly down and spilled milk flowed out from beneath the refrigerator, a finger of dirty white moving silently.

"King lemon picker. At least lemon picker for the day." Nick sat in the stern seat of the rubber raft while Toby worked the oars. "I was the only Anglo on the bus, sat way in back. Every day the foreman would ask how many boxes we'd picked. I was always lowest, till one day I just busted my butt and beat everybody. When I told the foreman my tally, all the braceros turned around and looked at me. My finest moment as a working man."

"Maybe you should have aimed a little higher," Nora said from her seat in the bow.

"Hey, follow your bliss, in the words of some idiot or another," Toby said and rowed a little harder.

The *Lily* lay at anchor on the south side of Noyes Island on a day of rest before the next opener. The wind had swung to the northwest and the sun was shining. The remnants of the swell broke on a long, flat beach. Toby had pumped up the rubber raft that Buddy kept in the lazarette, and Nick and Nora decided to go ashore with him. Buddy was napping in his bunk, and Danny had volunteered to stay aboard and watch that the anchor did not drag in the strong current that scoured the sandy bottom where they lay.

The three landed on a rocky promontory on the western end of the beach and dragged the raft to the drift pile above the high-water mark. The beach ran in a long arc, flat as a table, the sand dark and polished where touched by the cold hand of the waves. The offshore breeze blew spume backward from the long, curling shore break.

Toby took off his shoes and began to lope along the hard sand at the water's edge, dodging the reach of the waves. Nick and Nora beach-combed along the drift pile—bright bits of tattered nylon netting, a sneaker filled with sand, bottles with Japanese labels. Halfway down the beach, they stopped in the lee of a big drift log and sat on the warm sand. The day was cold enough to require a sweater, but the brilliant sun cooked the beach surface.

"Oh, man, this feels good." Nick lay on the hot sand and let the heat soak into his bones. "Every muscle in my body is sore." He shifted like an old dog on its favorite rug. "What I'm thinking, in Southeast, hot tubs should be filled with sand instead of water. There's enough water here already but there's a serious lack of dry. Think we could market the idea?"

"You might want to stick with lemon picking." Nora picked up a handful of sand and let it trickle though her fingers. She listened to the wind in the spruce trees, the thump of the surf, the hiss of blowing sand, the cry of gulls offshore. With one hand she dug a small hole; not far below the surface the sand became cold and damp and dark.

"It must be so cold on the bottom of the ocean," she said.

"You still on about that?"

"Last night I dreamed about Melody. One of those jumbled dreams where I was looking for her in Petersburg, then somehow we were on a boat and she was trying to tell me something but I couldn't make it out."

Toward Cape Addington mist poured across the hills, driven from the open ocean. The mist rolled downhill and then instantly disappeared about fifty feet above the water, gone as irrevocably as yesterday's dreams. Nora picked a beach pea, blew on the lavender blossom, and watched the wind take the petals across the sand. "I can't imagine dying that way, alone and scared. And everything so dark."

"Eternal rest grant unto her, oh Lord. And let perpetual light shine upon her."

"What's that from?"

"Mass for the Dead."

When they returned to the *Lily* they found that Danny had jigged up two halibut, about forty pounds each. "Something for the freezer," he said as he whetted a filleting knife on an oilstone.

Toby knelt and studied the fish, the mottled brown back, the white underbelly, and the two bulging eyes that had migrated to one side as the fish matured and flattened. "Amazing critters," he said. "Beautiful, really."

"Compared to what? Jayne fuckin' Mansfield?" Danny held the knifepoint against one of the fish and drew it slowly along the lateral line without breaking the skin. The dorsal fin rippled in reflex, a cresting wave that followed the knifepoint even after death.

When the fillets were cut, Danny propped a board on the deck divider. He held a fillet, skin side down, on the board and placed the edge of his knife between skin and flesh. With a single ripping motion, he pulled the skin free and tossed it overboard.

Nora fetched a pan from the galley. "Danny, what really happened?" she asked when they were alone.

"Say what?" Danny put the knife blade to another fillet.

"Melody. How did she go over? What was she doing on deck in the middle of the night?"

"Don't make it something it isn't." Danny ripped the skin free. "You ask me, if she didn't fall, then she jumped. Melody, she was pretty low, she might have bottomed out."

Two cormorants flew by, low and fast, dark black birds scrolling across the sky. They entered an even darker sea cave in a nearby cliff. Danny picked up one of the halibut carcasses and threw it overboard.

Nora watched it sink, dark head and tail connected by a bare white backbone, slipping sideways slowly down. A woman would never commit suicide that way, she thought, not going overboard in the dark from a fishing boat. Especially not if she was seasick.

"Well, what about the dealing?" she asked.

"The what?"

"Danny—"

Danny gestured with his knife. "Jesus, Nora, what's your problem? Fuckin' everybody in the fleet uses something."

"What were you peddling?"

"Pills, mostly—uppers. But some ganja, a little white lady. Why, you wanna buy something?"

"Yeah, right, the supermarket from hell."

Danny slammed his knife into the board. "Give me a fuckin' break. In the Bering Sea, we ate that shit like M&M's. You think you can go crabbing on cookies and milk?"

"But why sell to cannery workers? Kids, Danny."

"That wasn't supposed to be part of the deal." Danny bent and threw the second halibut overboard.

"Think those uppers had anything to do with Melody bottoming out?"

"Fuck me runnin'," Danny said angrily. They heard a chuff of noise and a sea lion broke water close to the boat, the halibut in its mouth. It shook its head, slamming the carcass on the water, tearing the skeleton to shreds.

CHAPTER 12

Warm Chuck Inlet, on the NW side of
Tonowek Bay, has considerable foul ground,
as indicated on the chart.

— US Coast Pilot

Three in the morning, the *Lily* pulled anchor and went around Cape Addington. Despite the dark, the waves were visible as they broke against the tumbled granite blocks of the cape. Hundreds of sea lions rested on the rocks; their rank, fishy odor palpable above the salt and diesel.

In the galley, Nora wore a heavy, shapeless sweater and a stocking cap. She stood close by the stove as the kettle came to boil. Danny had lifted the anchor, then fallen asleep on one of the benches, using his heavy coat as a blanket. Nick and Toby were still in their bunks.

Buddy was on the flying bridge. The roar dropped to a mutter as he put the engine in neutral. Nora looked out the galley door. They were just off the Haystack—Shaft Rock. It was still low water; Buddy must have opted to make their first set behind the usual hook-off.

Nora climbed the ladder to the bridge carrying two mugs of coffee in one hand. "Here," she said to Buddy. "I thought you might like this."

"Thanks, Nora. You could've stayed in bed another hour."

"I couldn't sleep." Nora watched the swell break against Shaft Rock in the first faint light of day. Buddy drew on his cigarette, and Nora sniffed the smoke. A long time since she had quit, but—early morning with a cup of coffee, that had always been the best cigarette of the day.

To the north, Nora could see the red and green lights of moving boats. She shivered at the touch of the breeze. Most seiners had enclosed bridges now. The newer boats were built that way and most of the older boats had been modified, but Milo had been too old school.

"Your dad, Milo, did he ever lose a crewman?" Nora asked.

"Lose?"

"I mean, drowned. You know, gone overboard."

"Nope. Dad, he sunk two boats, but he got everybody out both times."

"How about when he was running? Anybody ever fall over?"

"You're always afraid that'll happen. If somebody falls overboard when you're working the gear you can usually get 'em right back. But at night . . . they'd just be gone. I always check the bunks when I get up in the night."

Buddy flicked his cigarette butt over the side, a bright spark quickly extinguished. "I lost a crewman once, a kid. Boat rolled over and he got caught in the fo'c'sle. No way to get to him and then she went down. Pretty damn awful."

Nora blushed in the darkness. She had not meant to open old wounds. "It still bothers you?"

"Twenty years later I can still hear him pounding on the hull."

"But it happens. It could have happened to Milo. He was just lucky it never did."

"Luck, character, fate, who the hell knows. He was a nice kid too. From Kake. I haven't dared show my face there since."

"There must be two, three people from Kake drown every year."

"Yeah, but they're not my responsibility."

"Think it bothers Sven that much, losing Melody?"

"It should."

Danny was worried about Nora and her constant questions. He stood in the skiff, one hand on the wheel, towing hard against the current. He looked back at the long curve of the cork line, a beautiful, familiar shape. He was in a place he knew, doing something he was good at, but he felt edgy as a dog on a chain. If Nora stirred up a shit-storm, everybody was gonna get sprayed.

Why did she care anyway? She scarcely knew Melody. Danny had crewed with a guy named Andy who was similarly obsessed. Andy had been out in Togiak, herring fishing. Walking the beach before the opener, he had found a life raft in the drift pile. When he flipped it over there was a body tethered to it, from a crabber that had sunk with all hands near St. Paul Island that winter. Turned out the body was the boat cook, some young girl working to pay off college loans. One of the fishing newspapers ran a story with a picture from her high school yearbook. Andy just couldn't let it go; he clipped the picture and fastened it to his bunk, stared at it for hours. The girl had been a real beauty, but Danny knew what the body must have looked like after a couple of months in the Bering Sea. Maybe that was what haunted Andy—the contrast, like in some cheap horror movie.

Eventually Andy quit fishing and came ashore. Maybe he had found a real job, Danny didn't know. But Nora, she was such a pit bull; she was apt to worry it and worry it till the whole thing unraveled. Danny knew that if there was anything more than a perfunctory investigation he was in big trouble.

Fucking Sven and Melody, what a pair to draw to. Melody, she was the kind, sleeps with the skipper and figures she owns the boat. But Sven, he was like a dog with a rubber bone, pick it up, drop it, pick it up again. Slobber all over it and throw it away.

Buddy's soft voice came from the CB radio telling Danny to close up. Danny backed off on the throttle to gain some slack, then spun the wheel, put the hammer down, and began the long tow back to the *Lily*.

Not far north, Sara Quan was stacking web and thinking about heading south. She was tired of being cold, wet, and sleepless; it was time to be done with this fishing adventure. She pictured herself walking through Palo Alto in a summer dress, the sun shining, guys watching her.

Then a wolf eel, tangled in the net, came over the power block. Sara thought it was a kelp stem till it fell at her feet and writhed across the pile. She gave an inadvertent scream. Scott laughed and chucked the eel forward on the deck where it lay coiling and rippling. The energy was of fear, not malevolence, Sara realized, once her initial revulsion receded.

After the set, she went forward and hung her rain jacket on the peg, turned around and there was the eel a foot from her face—gray, bulbous head, needle-like teeth, writhing tail. She shrieked again. Scott held the eel by the head, brandishing it at her with an idiotic teenage grin. When the adrenaline faded Sara thought the eel had a more intelligent expression than Scott.

"Just throw it overboard," Aaron said disgustedly from where he was kicking fish into the hold.

Scott dropped the eel on the deck. The *Hero* was fully tanked and the deck was nearly awash. The wolf eel righted itself in a little rill of seawater, trying desperately to swim. It fetched up against a grated scupper and lay on its side gulping convulsively. Scott took a gaff hook and speared it through the head and threw it overboard, whirling to see how far he could throw it.

"Jesus, you didn't have to kill it," Sara said with a jolt of nausea at the senseless violence.

"It's only a fuckin' eel," Scott said, genuinely surprised.

The *Lily* anchored that night in Warm Chuck. Nora could see the processing barge *Arctic Star*, its high, blocky superstructure pockmarked with lights. People were moving on the working deck that was twenty feet above the water, and Nora could hear the groan and wail of hydraulics. The *Lily* was not scheduled to unload till morning, but Nora was too tired to sleep. She made a cup of tea and took it on the back deck. At this point of the season, a quiet moment alone was more precious than sleep.

She liked the crew well enough, except sometimes Danny, but she was so hungry for female companionship that she would even welcome a chat with Sara Quan. With the boys, there was never an open expression of emotion but always a barrage of irony and oblique wisecracks. As though conversation was a reverse poker game where only the losers revealed the cards they held.

The *Lily*'s generator was still running, chilling the fish. Buddy appeared and lowered a thermometer in the fish hold. He grimaced at the reading. As he bent over he kept one hand over his stomach. Nora had noticed that, no matter what she cooked, Buddy would just push the food around on his plate. He survived on an endless chain of cigarettes and candy bars.

Buddy disappeared in the direction of the engine room. Nora walked over to the rail. The deck lights illuminated a patch of water, green like the edge of plate glass. A school of squid came into view, drawn to the amphitheater of light. They pulsed gracefully as they moved, their tentacles billowing like dancer's skirts. Then, with a sudden spurt, they vanished. At the very edge of the circle of light a predatory shadow moved, flirting with the line of visibility. A coho, Nora thought. It faded back into obscurity and in a few minutes the squid entered again, stage right. They danced in unfathomable patterns, to unheard music, till Buddy killed the generator and the light died.

Pink bladders from gutted salmon festooned the enormous truck tires that the *Arctic Star* used as fenders. The *Lily* came alongside. Once she was secured, Toby and Nick pulled the hatch covers. A young Samoan wearing hip boots and a wife-beater T-shirt had come aboard from the *Star*, and he and Danny maneuvered the fish pump's suction hose into the hold. The hose could have been the trachea of a brontosaurus. Twenty feet above them, a crane controlled the hose, at its levers a big Samoan with a bushy Afro. His right arm bore a shark tattoo and the word "Mano."

When the pump started, Nora climbed the barge ladder carrying her shower gear. Newer boats like the *Viking Hero* had their own shower but not the *Lily Langtry*. On the work deck of the barge there was a sorting line much like the one in Petersburg. Looking down through a grating, Nora could see the slime line on the deck below. The crew appeared to be equal parts college kids, street people, and Filipinos. All wore blood-stained aprons, splattered with scales like sequins.

The showers were down a long corridor lined with doors, some bearing cartoons and magazine cutouts like a college dorm. Placards asked workers and visitors not to indulge in long showers, but even so, the hot water was blissful. When Nora finished, she set off in search of the cafeteria where Toby and Nick said they might go after the unloading. Confused by the maze of corridors, she headed down a ladder and came to an open workspace where Japanese technicians sorted fish eggs at manic speed. Nora looked around; she was not sure which way was forward and which was aft.

She caught a glimpse of Aaron from the *Viking Hero* disappearing around a corner. She followed him, lost him, then heard voices behind a row of stacked crates. She crept cautiously nearer, not sure why she was being surreptitious. Aaron was arguing vehemently with the Samoan with the shark tattoo. Aaron faced off in a truculent stance while the Samoan brandished a wad of bills. Nora could not make out what they were saying. She moved carefully closer, but a hand on her shoulder made her jump.

"Looking for something?" Sven asked.

"I was trying to find the cafeteria," Nora stammered. "I must have made a wrong turn."

"It's back aft. I'll show you." Sven took her arm and steered her away. Aaron and the Samoan watched them, the money no longer in evidence.

"I thought I was heading aft," Nora said. "I get turned around on these mid-decks." Up close Sven's bulk was intimidating.

"How do you like fishing with Buddy Stepovich?" he asked.

"We've caught a few fish. It's a good boat."

"It's Milo's boat," Sven snorted. "Milo's net, Milo's permit. Buddy's ridden those coattails all his life."

"Seems like we've outfished you a few times," Nora said tartly.

"The day Buddy Stepovich outfishes me I'll cut my own fuckin' throat." Sven held the cafeteria door for her but then turned away.

Nick and Toby and Sara Quan were sitting at a table. Nora had been anxious to talk with another woman, but now she wasn't sure.

"These old fishermen," Sara was saying, "they all look kind of mildewed, like a barrel of rotten apples."

"Decay, it's what the rain forest is all about," Toby said. "The trees, the buildings, the boats. Even the people. Sliding into nothingness together."

"The curve of equal time," Sara said.

"Say what?"

"It's a famous math problem. The shape of the curve, where, no matter where you start, you get to the bottom at the same time."

"Isn't that what a pendulum does?"

"A little more complicated than that. A tautochrone."

"I was just gettin' ready to say," Nick said with a wink at Nora. She shook her head, nothing on this barge made sense. On the wall behind Nick was a graph showing the barge's production of salmon cases during the Bristol Bay run. That was more like the math Nora knew—peaks and valleys and a summit you didn't know you'd reached till it was gone and you were already halfway down the back slope.

The door opened and Aaron walked into the cafeteria. He drew a cup of coffee from the urn and sat down at a nearby table. Greasy hair, a single earring, swirls of tattoos on his forearms; he studied Nora above the rim of his cup, his eyes as cold as a hawk's.

CHAPTER 13

Steamboat Bay, about 3 miles E. of Cape
Ulitka, is 0.8 mile wide at the entrance and
0.2 mile wide at the head. . . . At night, deep
shadows are cast by the mountains and the
entrance cannot always be readily distinguished.
                                    —US Coast Pilot

Sea anemones like huge cauliflowers clung to the fuel dock pilings. Danny filled the main tanks with diesel while Toby unrolled a hose and began to fill the water tank in the bow. The *Lily* lay in Steamboat Bay on the north end of Noyes Island. A series of tall red buildings with white barn-sash windows and cedar-shingled roofs stood close beneath the green wall of the rain forest. In bygone years Steamboat Bay had been an active cannery; now there was just the fuel dock, a small store, and an icehouse for the trollers.

"What are those for?" Toby pointed at logs the size of telephone poles that leaned like diagonal braces against the north wall of an adjacent building.

"Winter winds. I been in here with the urchin fleet when I thought the whole place was gonna come down like a house of cards. Southerlies come over that saddle like it's a venturi." Danny pointed south at a gap in the steep mountainsides.

When the tanks were full, they left the fuel dock and rafted outside a group of seiners tied to the main dock. Fishing would not open again for a day and a half, and Buddy had said they would spend the night in Steamboat. Danny wanted to check out a bar and grill that someone had opened on the ground floor of one of the old buildings. He and Toby climbed the ladder, bypassed a pickup basketball game, and came to a sign that said "Steamboat Café."

"Buy you a beer?" Danny asked.

"Maybe later. I want to climb the mountain."

Next to the caretaker's house a bit of surveyor's tape marked the beginning of a rudimentary trail. Pushing through the brush and devil's club, Toby quickly lost sight of any trail markers. He headed straight uphill, sometimes on his hands and knees.

Gnarled stands of dwarf juniper marked the tree line. Patches of snow lingered in the shaded corners of grassy meadows. Toby scrambled up a last steep pitch to the summit. The land fell sharply away to the west as though he rode the face of a cresting wave. Directly below was Roller Bay; serried ranks of surf broke fan-shaped on the white beach.

Toby lay back in the grass and stared at the sky, his head pillowed on his rucksack. He could hardly imagine that within the month he would be stuck in some classroom, discussing the imagery of redemption and loss in the Victorian novel—or some such. Back in the Lily's fo'c'sle he had a stack of required reading, books he had scarcely opened. On the fish boat there was always work for his hands or something in the ocean to enchant his eye and mind.

Danny was trying to convince him to stay for fall fishing and then maybe go longlining or even crabbing out of Dutch Harbor. One good crab season and he could pay all his school loans. Plus, Danny made the Bering Sea sound like a watery version of the Wild West—Dutch Harbor like Deadwood, with Wild Bill Hickok dealing poker in the back of the bar.

Staying north would also mean he would not have to watch Sara take up with some other guy. He did not relish the idea of seeing her arm in arm with somebody like that blond tennis player she used to date.

Toby had spent all his life in college towns. Maybe it was time for a change of scenery. He looked east, across the Gulf of Esquibel. Far away he saw the splash of a whale breaching. The whale jumped again and then again and then the sea was still.

"It's a netting loft," Nora said. "Guys from Craig must still come out here. It's big enough you can hang a ten fathom stretch at a whack." She and Nick were on the second floor of one of the old cannery buildings. Huge pillars of Douglas fir framed an open expanse that ran the length of the building, about eighty feet. From the ceiling bits of string dangled, terminating in bent wire hooks.

"Looks like a ballroom," Nick said. The floor was clean except for a few bits of lacing twine, the boards polished by the miles of web that fishermen had dragged across.

"It's a lot of work hanging a seine. You hang the lead and cork lines from those hooks, then lace the strips of web together. It feels like it's miles long." She remembered winter days at the old Harbor Seafood cannery in Wrangell, fishermen bundled against the cold while they hung seines, their netting needles flashing in the gloom.

She and Nick climbed another set of stairs to the third floor. There were no windows on this floor. A single string of overhead lights showed rows of gear lockers—chicken wire enclosures with pad-locked doors. The dust lay heavy and undisturbed on long-forgotten stacks of cork line and bundles of web. Boat names were painted on the locker doors—*Ranger, Rachel Colleen, Haida Girl.*

"I remember those boats from the old days. They're mostly gone now," Nora said. She pointed to a locker with the name *Mary Eileen.* "Buddy's old boat, the one that sank." Behind the door there was a bronze snatch block and a bright orange buoy with "Stepovich" painted on it.

"Danny told me there was a regular bunch used to fish this coast years ago," Nick said. "The Haystack Gang. All high-line fishermen. Buddy was the youngest. I guess he was the rising star."

"Where is he tonight?"

"On the boat. Was he always that much of a lone wolf?"

"Back in Wrangell, he was always aloof," Nora said, "but alone at the center of the crowd, you know what I mean? I never could figure him out, and now it's like he's disappeared even further into himself. All those lost years."

"Dreams die hard." A path Nick understood. "I dunno why, but it reminds me of something years ago. I was headed north to Fairbanks and stopped at this bar in Whitehorse. There was a couple playing shuffleboard—that bar game with the red and green pucks? The guy was Indian, maybe midthirties, wearing cowboy boots and a western shirt. Kind of drunk. But his lady friend, she was something else entirely. A white woman in her forties, blonde turning gray. She was wearing a formal dress. I mean full tilt—flouncy floor-length skirt, low top with spaghetti straps. And a rhinestone tiara."

"My long-lost twin sister," said Nora. "I wondered where she'd got to."

"But you had to wonder what was the curve of her life," Nick said. "How did she end up in a backstreet bar in a rhinestone tiara?"

"Same thing that got us here."

Nick studied the left-behind gear in the lockers. "Danny offered to help me fix up the *Guinevere*. He's got this plan for us to go pot shrimping on the *Lily* and meanwhile work on the *Guinevere*."

"Us?"

"Me and him and Buddy, and maybe Toby, only Toby's got this jones to go crabbing out west."

"Toby? What about school?"

"It can wait. I guess some boats are making huge scores out there."

"Jesus, I can't believe it," Nora said. "If he even considers joining this merry band of losers, I'll kill him myself."

The shadows climbed to the alpine meadow where Toby slept. He awoke from his nap and stretched, stiff and cold. He started down the hill, but in the gloom beneath the tall trees he veered too far south and lost his way. Eventually he came to a small stream that he followed downward, clambering over fallen trees in the brush-choked gully, his face scratched, his shirt ripped.

At the bottom, he ducked beneath the leathery leaves of a red cedar and found himself on a stretch of shingle beach. In the dark waters of the creek mouth he saw the furtive movement of a small fish, perhaps a sculpin. Half a mile north was the Steamboat cannery.

When he reached the boardwalk he was drawn to the light and noise of the Steamboat Café. He had a few dollars in his pocket, enough to buy two bottles of Red Hook from a barmaid named Kelp. Toby drained one beer at a gulp and looked around the crowded room. Danny was huddled with that guy Aaron; Billy Nichols was trying to chat up the pretty cook from the *Velvet*. No one registered Toby's presence. He took his second beer outside to a bench by the now empty basketball court. Someone climbed the ladder from the moored boats and headed his way. Sara.

"Miss Q.," said Toby.

"You look like you've been mugged," said Sara.

"You should see the other guy." But had the mountain even registered his presence?

Sara sat down beside him. "Give me a drink of your beer." She reached for the bottle and took a swig. She was wearing woolly black tights and a clean white shirt that was unbuttoned to show a bit of black brassiere. Her hair was freshly washed, and she had even put on eyeliner. For whom was she trolling, dressed so provocatively? During Sara's first weeks on the *Viking Hero*, Toby had scarcely recognized her in baggy sweats and T-shirts. She must have found her bearings and was now looking to cause a little trouble.

"You seen Aaron or Billy?" she asked.

"They were in the bar a couple minutes ago."

"Sven's got this hard-on to leave like right now, and I'm supposed to round them up. He could have told us earlier. What an asshole. Three more openings and I'm outta here." She took another swig of beer—somehow it had become her bottle, a typical Sara move, but Toby said nothing.

"You made your ticket home yet?" she asked.

"Actually I'm thinking of staying for fall fishing."

"What about school?"

"I might drop out for a year. Go out to Dutch Harbor and see what that's all about."

"Oh, boy. Real man syndrome."

"Knock it off, Sara."

"Sorry." She opened her dark eyes widely—little girl instantly contrite—but Toby wasn't buying that either. They sat silently, something awkward and unspoken between them, like a reunion of opposing sides from a long-ago war.

"What was that 'curve of equal time' stuff you were on about at the barge?" Toby asked.

"Famous geometry problem in the seventeenth century. Pascal offered a big prize for a solution. One of the Bernoulli brothers figured it was like a cycloid curve."

"What's that when it's among friends?"

"Close your eyes." Sara put one hand over his eyes and rested the other lightly on his chest. "Now, picture that night we were walking along the railroad tracks and saw a boxcar with a glowing spot on its wheel."

"A hotbox." Mostly he remembered the touch of her hands in other times, other places.

"If you map its path, you've got a cycloid—a point on a circle rolling along a straight line." She left her hand over his eyes for a moment, then drew it away, letting her fingertips trail lightly down his cheek. "Understand that much?"

"The heart has its own reasons, which reason does not know," Toby said.

"What's that? One of your dipshit poets?"

"Pascal. After he gave up math for higher pursuits."

"Touché. C'mon, help me find those two bozos." She grabbed Toby's hands and pulled him to his feet. Linking her arm in his, she steered him to the door.

Toby caught a strong whiff of perfume from Sara's glossy hair. Looking down he could see the soft swell of her breasts in the open blouse. The curve of unquenchable desire. He knew Sara was playing a game with him, trying to see how deeply the hook was still set, but the minute she had touched him he had become erect and he was sure she was aware of that. The prick has no conscience, and not much in the way of judgment either.

Aaron and Billy were not in the bar. Sara drew Toby over to the building that housed the netting loft. On the ground floor near the ice plant, a cone of light from an overhead lamp showed two men talking angrily—Aaron and Danny. Aaron shoved Danny roughly, and Danny spun against one of the pillars, giggling uncontrollably, obviously very drunk.

"That fuckin' Mano wouldn't pay full price, said you owed him," Aaron said. "What the fuck's that all about, Daniel?"

Danny held up his hands in a mocking gesture of non-comprehension. Aaron grabbed him by the shirtfront, pulled a sheath knife, and held it to Danny's throat. "You little shit—"

Toby made a startled exclamation and started toward them, but Sara's hand tightened on his arm. "Aaron," she said sharply. "Sven wants us on the boat. Now." She let go of Toby and took a step away.

Aaron turned as she spoke, showing no surprise at their presence. He put his knife back in the sheath. "What the fuck for?" he said.

"He wants to anchor outside."

"Fuckin' prick."

"You know where Billy is?"

Aaron shook his head slowly, studying them both. Toby took a step toward him, his feet spread, braced, his fists clenched. Aaron locked eyes with him momentarily and then walked by, ignoring Sara, and just brushing Toby with his shoulder as he passed. Toby spun around.

"Tobias," Sara said softly but firmly.

Toby looked at her, then turned to Danny. "You all right?"

"It's time to leave her, Johnny, leave her," Danny sang. "Time to leave 'er like a man." He hiccoughed and said, "Old sea chantey. You seen my beer? I had nearly a full bottle." He looked around and his eyes focused on Sara.

"Sara Quan," he said, "pleased to make your acquaintance." Still leaning against the pillar, he extended his hand formally and they shook, but Danny kept hold of her hand.

"Holy shit," he said, "you're prettier than my mother's picture."

Danny let go and slid slowly down the pillar to sit spraddle-legged on the floor. "Actually," he said, "my mother was ugly as a stump." He fell over on his side and began to snore.

Toby let out his breath in a whistle of released tension.

"Your problem now, sweetheart." Sara kissed the fingers of her left hand and touched them gently to his lips, then turned and ran after

Aaron. Her white shirt glimmered in the shadows like the wings of a moth. Toby caught one more glimpse of her through the windows as she ran down the alleyway toward the boats.

CHAPTER 14

Cape Bartolome, the S extremity of Baker Island,
has several storm-swept islets, some partly wooded,
off the main shore. . . . The cape rises rather sharply.
— US Coast Pilot

"By-the-wind sailors," Danny said. He leaned over the rail to look at a fleet of tiny jellyfish. Toby scooped one up with a fine mesh net and laid it carefully on deck. It was translucent, a blue-lavender disk about four inches across with a wing two inches high set aslant. How could jelly be shaped to catch the wind?

"They don't show up often, but when they do it's a crowd," Danny said. "They even tack together."

"Where do they go?"

"Wherever the wind takes them." Danny eyes were red-rimmed, and his hands shook slightly after his night in the bar. The *Lily* lay in the bight by the Haystack, the afternoon before the opening.

"Jesus, that's beautiful." Toby gently touched the clear sail. "Let the wind decide. Not a bad way to live." He carefully returned the tiny creature to the sea and watched it bob away with the rest of the armada. "By-the-wind sailor. I'm gonna look 'em up in Ricketts." He headed for the galley and his copy of *Between Pacific Tides*, the closest thing to poetry on the boat.

In the galley Nora was making a coffee cake. She cut the lid off a two pound can of honey, took the lid to the back deck, and tossed it overboard. She watched it turn over and over as it sank, flashing like a navigation marker as it caught the light. The flash grew fainter and disappeared. Farewell to the sun.

She walked over to Danny and said in a low voice, "Daniel Sullivan, if you talk that boy into quitting school I'll cut your balls off and use them for halibut bait."

"Hey, he's a grownup."

"No, he's not. What's going on with those Samoans?"

"Those what?" The curveball caught Danny unawares.

"On the *Arctic Star*. I saw Aaron with one. And Sven. Money was changing hands."

"Oh, yeah. Probably Mano, or his brother." Danny waved his hand dismissively.

"Daniel . . ."

Danny let out his breath slowly. He was tired of Nora's questions, but he knew she would badger him relentlessly. "Mano, I knew him from Dutch; he was our connection."

"Connection?"

"The plan was we'd only sell to dealers like Mano, not put the stuff on the street ourselves. Safer that way, only Aaron got risky."

"You were all in on it?"

"Aaron got the crank and the other stuff from some guys we knew in the slam. I was the one who supposedly knew the market. Melody and Billy, they weren't in on it, but you couldn't very well keep it secret on a fifty-eight-foot boat."

"And Sven?"

"He bankrolled it."

"But why? That's the part I don't get. Sven makes plenty of money."

"To hear him talk he's more broke than any of us. Got hammered in his divorce."

"As he so richly deserved."

"Whatever. But he figures somebody owes him. Plus, guys are building bigger boats all the time, and he wants a new one. You know skippers—biggest dick syndrome."

"I still don't get it. Why the risk, Danny? I mean, you're still on probation, right? You really want to go back to prison?"

"Look, you saw Eigil. Past forty and not a pot to piss in. He can still do the work, but how much longer? Five years? Ten? Then he's down on his knees beggin' work from some pissant skipper half his age. You think that's not a prison?"

"Danny, Danny . . ." Nora said, but Danny looked away, toward the wind-twisted trees atop the dark cliffs.

"What were you and Danny Sullivan arguing about?" Sara asked Aaron while fishing the next day.

"Nothing."

"Nothing?" Sara remembered the drawn knife.

"Just a bar argument we took outside. Danny, he has a few drinks, he can be a real prick." Aaron looked at her with that odd downturned grin that reminded her of a skate she had seen hanging in a fishmonger shop in Chinatown, a diamond-shaped fish, with a barbed tail and a mouth like a curved slash across its white belly.

Sara yawned. Jesus, she needed about a week of sleep.

"Long day ahead, sissy."

"Gimme." Sara extended her hand.

Aaron grinned and took a bottle from his pocket and shook two pills into her open palm. Sara swallowed them and leaned back against the sink, arms folded, waiting for the rush. Aaron watched her; she felt like a bird caught in the gaze of a bull snake, but then her blood started to race and she knew she could handle any situation. Where did he get off calling her sissy?

"Have you got a girlfriend?" she asked.

"Nobody special."

"Not ever?"

"I was married once. First time I went to the pen she sent me my walking papers."

"Childhood sweethearts?"

"You wanna call it that. We grew up in the same trailer court. Started diddlin' each other in the bushes when she was like fourteen and I was sixteen. Turns out my old man was doin' her old lady at the same time."

"How romantic."

"She got knocked up, and I got married at seventeen. My daughter, same thing, pregnant at fifteen. I got a grandkid in Winslow, Arizona, I've never seen."

"Never seen?" Sara wished Aaron didn't have such bad teeth. And eyes like a ratfish, green and blank as marbles. Those eyes pinned her now, and she was no longer sure she was in control.

Fishing was poor that day. On a hunch, Buddy took the *Lily* south, toward Baker Island. A line of eight or ten boats fished off Granite Point, but the *Lily* passed them by.

"That's a famous hook-off," Danny said of Granite Point. "Craig boats fish there but only Indian boats. A White boat shows up, they'll cork it."

"How come?"

"It's just always been that way."

"What's corking?" Nick asked.

"Setting your gear right in front of another boat so they've got no room to fish."

The second day of the opening they fished inside Cape Bartolome, just offshore of a big sea lion rookery. A solitary bull made himself at home in the back of their net, surfacing about thirty fathoms from the *Lily*'s stern with a big coho clamped in his jaw.

Nick had been attempting to juggle three busted corks that had been stripped from the net. When the sea lion dove, he said to Nora, "Bet you a steak dinner I can hit that sea lion with a cork."

"You're on," Nora said. They were all a bit punchy from lack of sleep.

Nick stood at the rail with his arm cocked, watching the line of red corks. The sea lion resurfaced and Nick whipped his arm down. The cork flew straight as a string and bounced off the startled sea lion's head.

"Cheater," Nora giggled, though she didn't know why.

"Major league arm," said Toby.

"Not really," said Nick. "Sometimes from deep third I had to bounce the ball. You should have seen this shortstop I played with in the minors, Ray Oyler. Skinny guy but he had an arm like a buggy whip. Couldn't hit at all, though. It was pathetic to watch him swing a bat. Pathetic. But he made it to the big leagues."

In the middle of the strait, a pod of killer whales appeared, their dorsal fins standing tall like the masts of a fleet of warships. In a flurry of panic, the sea lions all headed for shore, the one in the *Lily's* net going over the cork line in a slash of movement.

Nick picked up a gaff, tossed a cork in the air, and swung at it, smooth and easy. The cork went high and deep, a red dot against the sky, falling just short of the cork line that curved like an outfield wall. Fifteen feet farther, Nick thought. If I could have hit the ball just fifteen feet farther.

CHAPTER 15

*Craig is an incorporated settlement on Prince of
Wales Island at the S end of Klawock Inlet and
close SE of Fish Egg Island.*

—US *Coast Pilot*

Craig on a cloudy afternoon: dusty streets, pickup trucks, barking
dogs—civilization. Nora joined the long queue at the harbor pay
phones. When her turn came, she dialed Trish's number, but the
phone rang for a long time before she answered.

"'Lo," Trish said, her voice subdued.

"Hi, honey."

"Mom . . . ? Mom? Where are you?"

"In Craig, on Prince of Wales Island. I haven't been able to get to a
phone. We've been fishing hard."

"I wondered why I hadn't heard from you." Trish gave a little sigh.
"So how's it going?"

"Pretty good." Nora hesitated. "Is anything wrong?"

"No, nothing."

"Is Duane there?"

"No, he took off in my car a little while ago. His pickup's broke
down like always."

Nora thought that if Duane never came back, losing the car would
be a cheap price to pay, but there was something else in Trish's voice.
"What's the matter, baby?" she asked.

"Mom, I'm six weeks late. I think I'm pregnant."

"Oh dear. Oh dear. Did you take one of those drugstore tests?"

"I'm afraid to."

"Have you told Duane?"

"Mom, I think he's seeing someone else." Trish started to cry quietly.

"Oh, sweetheart," Nora said, clutching the receiver so hard her knuckles whitened. So many things she wanted to say but none of them mattered. The two talked in disjointed fashion till Trish became racked by sobs and hung up. Nora put the receiver back and stood there thinking till the fisherman behind her in line cleared his throat.

"Jesus Goddamn Moses," Nora said, startling the guy. She strode down to the harbor, mad at Duane, mad at every man in the world. The high bows of the moored boats looked down on her.

Later she and Nick headed for Ruth Ann's Restaurant. After her phone call Nora had almost begged off dinner, but she was hungry and she needed to get off the boat. They were going reverse Dutch treat; Nick insisted that nothing in their bet precluded him from buying her dinner.

The back room at Ruth Ann's overlooked the water. The room was undergoing renovation; the carpenters were gone for the day, but a table saw stood in the middle of the room. A typically Alaskan approach to fine dining, Nora thought. They both ordered steaks.

"Danny told me a strange story," Nick said. "About a mass murder that happened right out there." He pointed south. "Fish Egg Island, I think he said."

"The *Investor*. It was in the newspapers a lot."

"Seven people killed? Maybe eight? The captain, the crew, even the captain's wife and little kids."

"And the wife was pregnant." Nora grimaced. "The bastard shot them, then opened the sea cocks. Only the boat didn't sink so he went back the next day and set fire to it. In full view of Craig on a summer day."

"Danny said they put some guy on trial."

"A former crewman, but he was acquitted. No hard evidence, I guess. Plus, he got some loud-mouthed lawyer."

"The whole story's so strange," Nick said.

"It's funny country up here. So big and empty that a lot of stuff falls through the cracks. The law is like a net with meshes that are too big."

"I was amazed when I went to work for Buddy and didn't have to sign a tax form or give a social security number or anything. It's like nobody cares. Why bother even filing your taxes?"

"A lot of guys don't."

Early evening now, a small outboard skiff went by, its wake rolling gold in the slanting sun. Nick poured Nora a second glass of wine.

"You talk to your daughter?" he asked.

"Yeah."

"How was she?"

"Pregnant."

Nick cut another bit of steak and chewed it meditatively. "I take it this was not entirely good news."

"It wasn't planned, if that's what you mean. Plus, the guy's a total jerk."

"They're not married?"

"No."

"Is she going to have it?"

"I don't know, I couldn't ask. Nick, I don't know what to tell her. Her own father was a jerk, and she wasn't planned either. I got married because I was pregnant and maybe if abortion had been legal back then Trish would never have had the opportunity to find out how fucked up life can be." Nora stopped for breath and stared at what remained of her T-bone.

"Man born of woman has a short time to live, full of misery. He springs up like a flower and is cut down."

"What's that from?"

"Paul's epistle to the Corinthians. More or less."

"Were your parents church people?" Toby had once mentioned how much Catholicism shaped Nick's conversation; Nora had never paid much attention.

"My mother, for sure. She'd go to early Mass four, five times a week, no matter the weather. My dad, not so much, but they were both just deeply good people. Principled, you know. I was lucky, the amount of love they gave me."

"What would they think of you now?" Nora said and then wished she could bite her tongue off.

Sara looked through her locker and pulled out a clean pair of jeans and a black and silver top, brief enough to show a bit of midriff. Billy had said there was a band playing at the Craig Inn. He and Scott had left the boat an hour ago. Aaron was in his bunk, reading yet another gun magazine.

Sara started to carry her change of clothes to the head but then thought, what the hell, and pulled off her sweatpants and stepped into her jeans with her back turned toward Aaron. She moved quickly, as though she had forgotten he was there, but she could feel his eyes rake her back and legs and a bit of a smile crossed her lips.

She ran a comb through her hair. She felt oddly jagged; her brain seemed to be firing in fits and starts, like an engine that needed tuning. The first time Aaron had offered her a couple of those little red pills, she had been reluctant to take them, but it had been the second day of a tough opener and she was running on empty. Now she could not imagine making it through an opener without a little boost. Once she was off the boat that would be the end of the drugs, but this was her summer to run a little wild.

Aaron sat up on the edge of his bunk and packed his bong. He put a small piece of what looked like a salt crystal on top of the weed and lit the pipe.

"I thought we were going dancing," Sara said.

"What's the rush?" Aaron took a long hit, then proffered the pipe to Sara.

"What is it?" she asked.

"You'll like it, princess. Trust me."

"Yeah, right," she said but took the pipe. She didn't want Aaron to think she was afraid of anything. She took a drag, coughed raggedly, took another. She shrugged noncommittally and passed the pipe back to Aaron. But then a big snake of fire grabbed the base of her spine and coiled up to flare in her brain like a cobra spreading its hood.

"Holy fuck," she said.

"Hey, white man, come have a drink with me." Danny nudged Toby with his boot.

"Whaaat . . ." Toby sputtered. He had lain down in his bunk with a book and had instantly fallen into a sodden, heavy sleep. He looked at the watch taped to the bulkhead by his bunk. It said 8:30, presumably p.m.

"C'mon, kid, it's our one night in town."

"Yeah, sure," Toby yawned.

"Where's Nick?" Danny looked at the empty bunks.

"He and Nora went to dinner."

"Are they becoming a number?"

"I don't think even they know."

Together Danny and Toby walked up the dock. "What's up with that white man stuff?" Toby asked.

"When I was nineteen I worked on a Craig seiner, the *Libby 6*," Danny said. "I was the only white guy on the boat and whenever we were in town, if I tried to sleep, somebody would holler down the fo'c'sle, 'Hey, white man, come up and drink with us.'"

"Charming," Toby said. He took a deep breath of salt air to clear his mind. A block from the Craig Inn they could already hear the heavy beat of a bass guitar.

The poster outside the bar said the band was from Los Angeles. But all bar bands were from LA, by way of Fargo, North Dakota, Toby thought. The band was two guitars and a keyboard. One of the guitarists, a Black guy, doubled on a sax that had an electronic pickup right in its bell. The noise was deafening. Across the crowded dance floor Toby saw Sara at a table with Aaron and her other crewmates. Danny bought two beers and they found a table. Toby turned his chair so that he would not have to watch Sara.

The bandleader announced a twenty-minute break and the noise lessened. Toby felt a hand on the back of his neck.

"Where were you guys?" Sara Quan said. "I looked for you at the barge."

"We unloaded to a tender," Danny said.

"Didja hear? The barge is leaving tomorrow. Not enough fish, so we're gonna have to deliver to Petersburg."

"Buy you a drink?" Danny offered.

"Sure." Sara sat down on Toby's lap. "We've been drinking rusty nails."

"What's a rusty nail?" Toby asked.

"Scotch and Drambuie." Sara began to massage Toby's neck, and he couldn't resist putting his hand on her thigh. A perfect fit. Danny returned from the bar with a rusty nail and two more beers. Sara took a drink, making sure her hair brushed Toby's face. Then she put the glass down and took a swig of Toby's beer.

"This other stuff doesn't quench your thirst," she said. She tried to put the bottle to Toby's lips but he flinched away. "Tobias, we were having an argument about the Drambuie bottle. Where it says 'a link with the '45'? Aaron says it's about guns, like a Colt .45. I told 'em you'd know."

"It's Scottish history. The Jacobite rebellion in 1745. Bonny Prince Charlie."

"I thought it was from record players," Danny said. "Forty-five rpm, like those old doo-wop records."

"Nope. The clans invaded England, but the generals bungled it, and the Highlanders were butchered at Culloden."

"Were any of your MacGregor ancestors there?" Sara asked teasingly. "Like the famous Rob Roy?"

"Rob Roy was dead and the whole clan was outlawed." Toby's Scots blood began to boil. He took his hand off Sara's leg. "Couldn't speak the name, couldn't wear the tartan."

"You mean those things like skirts? They really wore them? No wonder you guys ended up a bunch of limp-dick professors."

Toby didn't bother to explain the difference between the kilt and the tartan. He stood up abruptly, dumping Sara on the floor. She got up and dusted her pants, not at all disconcerted. To Danny, Toby said, "Gotta go, thanks for the beers." Carrying his last beer, he pushed his way through the crowd. The band had returned to the stand, the

Black guy playing a riff on the saxophone, a bit of Coltrane, perhaps to remind himself he could play something other than "Louie, Louie."

Out on the darkened streets Toby finished his beer and slam dunked the bottle in a trash can, where it shattered on impact. What was up with Sara? That glittering, brittle look in her eyes. All his time with her, she had never lost control.

The walk to the harbor cooled his temper. At the top of the ramp a young crewman was shouting into a pay phone. "Goddamnit, this is the third time I've called. It's after midnight and where the fuck are you?" The guy slammed the phone down so hard it jumped off the hook. He strode away, leaving the receiver swinging on its cord.

Tough, having to talk to an answering machine, Toby thought. The wind had risen and the moored boats stirred restlessly. Was this his life now? When he reached the *Lily* he could see Nick and Nora sitting at the galley table, talking. Rather than having to speak with them, Toby climbed on the foredeck and went down to the fo'c'sle via the forward hatch. He lay on his bunk, sleepless in the dark.

Sara danced on in the crowded bar. Aaron was a good dancer, kind of slow and languid. He would seem to be a bit behind the beat but then suddenly right on tempo, snakelike.

Caught in the whirl of sound and shadow, Sara shaped her moves to his. She did not notice the crowd thinning, scarcely noticed the band packing its instruments. Aaron took her arm and steered her past the tables littered with beer bottles. The floor was sticky with spilled beer and dust. When they reached the street, Sara breathed deeply.

"Wow, night," she said as if she had never seen it before. A few other figures were weaving toward the harbor. "C'mon, dance with me," she said to Aaron. "I can still hear the music." She grabbed his hands and began to swing but slipped and nearly fell. Aaron caught her by the waist.

"Easy, sissy," he said. He put an arm under her shoulder, his big hand across her bare midriff beneath the swell of her breasts. He bent and kissed her hard, his other hand on her backside. Sara was halfway into the kiss before she even realized what was happening. She relaxed for a moment and kissed him back but then broke away.

"Naughty, naughty," she said but still leaned against him as they walked down the float. On one boat a crewman leaned over the rail puking, which Sara thought was unbelievably funny.

The *Viking Hero* was rafted outside three other boats. Her lights were ablaze and her main engine was running. "Jesus Christ," Aaron muttered as he helped Sara across the other boats, "I can't believe that asshole wants to leave now."

"That's Captain Asshole to you, boy," Sara said, drawing herself upright and saluting.

"Hey, pipe down."

"Of the good ship Fucking Zero." Sara laughed merrily.

"Where the fuck have you been?" Sven shouted as he came out of the dark wheelhouse. "Cut her loose and let's get out of here."

Grumbling under his breath Aaron went forward to release the bow mooring line. Sara headed aft, leaning on the chained skiff, and undid the stern line. With the screw churning in reverse, the boat backed away. Sara pulled up the fender and stumbled forward across the seine pile. She looked back at the harbor lights; they were oddly doubled. She left the mooring lines and fenders for Aaron to stow and headed for the fo'c'sle.

Billy and Scott were asleep in the upper bunks. The noise and vibration of the engine sent a wave of nausea through Sara and her high collapsed, leaving her in a desolate place. The scotch and beer in her stomach rolled as though it felt the pull of the tide. Her clothing stank of beer and cigarettes. She needed a shower. She stripped off her jeans and shirt and pulled on the baggy shirt she wore as a nightgown. She was bent over looking in her locker for shampoo when she felt Aaron's weight pressing against her. He put his hands on her hipbones and pulled her hard against him till she could feel the bulge in his pants.

"Hey, knock it off," she said, but Aaron spun her around and pinned her up against the bunk. He kissed her, forcing his tongue between her lips. For a moment her muscles relaxed and she opened her mouth wide and kissed him deeply, their tongues tangling, but she could taste cheap scotch and rotten teeth and she broke off and tried to push him away. "Enough," she said, but Aaron tried to kiss her again, his hands hard on her arms, his mouth seeking hers as she tried to twist away.

"Quit it," she yelled.

Billy rolled over and said sleepily, "You two want to keep it down?"

Aaron ran his hand beneath her shirt and Sara tried to slap him but he backheeled her, knocking her into her bunk. He leaned on her, his left forearm across her collarbone while his right hand tweaked her nipples. She twisted frantically and clasped her knees together as he tried to insinuate his leg between them. Aaron switched his grip. One hand across her mouth while the other went for her crotch. She felt the harsh scrape of his fingernails inside her. The anger in his eyes turned her muscles to water, but she tried to bite the hand that was forcing her head back into the mattress. She felt him unbuckle his belt with one hand and pull at his zipper.

"Aaron," someone said sharply. Aaron turned slightly, and Sara could see Sven in the doorway behind him. "Your watch," Sven said and jerked his thumb over his shoulder.

Aaron stood up and buckled his belt. He gave Sara a cold look and left the fo'c'sle without a word. Sara pulled her shirt down to cover herself and shrank back in her bunk, still shaking with fear and disbelief. Sven looked at her huddled in her bunk, shook his head disgustedly, and turned away.

When both men were gone, Sara grabbed her towel and bolted for the head. She locked the door, knelt, and retched violently in the toilet. She clung to it for a moment, then rose and turned on the shower full blast. Noticing the tiny porthole above the basin she almost screamed at the thought of an arm reaching through it. She dogged the porthole tightly shut, then stood under the shower and scrubbed herself relentlessly.

Sara stayed locked in the head for more than an hour, growing colder by the minute but afraid to leave. Finally, she summoned the courage to open the door a crack. The galley was dark and the fo'c'sle as well. Sven's door was closed. She took a tentative step to where she could see up the companionway to the flying bridge. A faint greenish light from the radar illuminated a bit of ceiling as though she were looking up a mineshaft at the northern lights.

Sara ran to the fo'c'sle, jumped in her bunk, and drew the makeshift curtain. She huddled beneath her blankets, hard against the hull. She could feel the heavy thrum of the diesel.

CHAPTER 16

Kelly Cove, on the W side of St. Nicholas Channel,
0.6 mile from Point Santa Theresa, affords anchorage
for small craft in 6 to 9 fathoms, rocky bottom.
—US Coast Pilot

Sara awoke from an uneasy doze. She lay in her bunk listening to the anchor chain grind in the chocks while the *Viking Hero* rolled wickedly. She peeked out from behind her curtain. No one was moving, she quietly rose and headed for the galley. Everyone else was asleep.

She stood at the sink drinking glass after glass of water. As the boat rolled, it dipped the through-hull drainpipe and the kitchen sink gurgled at her bestially. She had not felt seasick since the first week, but now she was hungover, exhausted, frightened. On top of that, she felt the sort of mealy backache that always presaged her period. Moon-driven, in lockstep with the tides.

Thinking that fresh air might help, she went out on deck. The *Hero* lay at anchor in the bight near the Haystack. One other boat was there, an old seiner tucked way back in the kelp with stabilizers out; her anchor chain slackened and tightened as her bow rose to the waves. The *Hero* had anchored farther from shore and was caught in the trough so that she nearly dipped her rail with each wave. Saltwater burst through the scuppers and soaked Sara to the knees.

She looked out to sea: gray skies, gray humpbacked waves, a gray horizon made fuzzy by the heaving sea. A wave broke on a nearby rock and white foam seethed through the popweed. Sara leaned over the rail and vomited, her long hair snarling in the wind. She felt weak, hot, and clammy, but also shaking from the chill air. She ducked back in the galley. She had left her glass of water on the counter, and despite the nonskid matting it had flown off and broken on the galley floor. A plate had fallen from its cubbyhole above the sink and broken as well. Sven stood surveying the wreckage.

"Clean this shit up," he said then turned away.

After picking up the broken glass and mopping the floor, Sara took a Dramamine and returned to her bunk and put her pillow over her head. She heard the main engine start. Aaron left his bunk and soon after the anchor chain began to rattle in. Half an hour later the boat's motion suddenly eased.

Little Roller Bay, Sara thought. For once Sven had been sensible enough to seek calmer waters. The anchor dropped again, and she fell into a deep sleep.

A hand shook her awake. She rolled violently away from the touch. "The boys are hungry," Sven said. "That's your job, remember?"

Sara climbed out of her bunk, still feeling sick. Cigarette smoke was thick in the galley, coating her skin. Scott and Billy sat at the table playing cribbage; Aaron was nowhere in sight. Sara took four rib-eye steaks from the refrigerator. Red meat, that was all the crew ever wanted, but at least it was quick. Blood showed against the wrinkled shrink-wrap, and she tore the plastic off and poured the excess down the drain, fighting a tide of nausea.

She found the salad fixings and was beginning to chop an avocado when the engine room door opened, sending a sharp pulse of diesel noise and odor into the room. Aaron appeared and took a beer from the refrigerator. He snapped the cap while casually raking Sara with his eyes. She felt a trickle of sweat roll down her side.

"About time you showed up," he said.

Sara did not reply. Her hands were trembling, and she dropped the knife and clasped her arms around her to hide her fear.

"What the fuck's your problem?" Aaron said, exasperated. He kept his voice low and his back to the table, which shielded their conversation from Scott and Billy but also pinned Sara in a corner.

"I said no. That's all I have to say. You should have stopped." Sara remembered his hand inside her and the bitter chyme rose and burned in her throat.

"You stupid cunt," Aaron hissed and grabbed her arm, hard. "You said no? You said no? You've been shaking your ass at me for a month and then all of a sudden it's no?" A fleck of spittle hit her face. He yanked her arm so hard she nearly fell, but then he turned away and walked onto the back deck, slamming the door behind him.

Uppity fuckin' cunt, Aaron fumed to himself as he lit a cigarette. He should've reamed her good. And that prick Sven calling him off, like he was a dog to the leash. That was the last time he'd let Sven get away with that crap. He'd had about all he could take of this boat bullshit. No one told him what to do, not ever.

Back in the galley Sara wiped her face clean. She should have kicked Aaron in the balls, screamed, done anything, but she had been so frozen that she hadn't even flinched. She picked up the knife and tried again to slice the avocado, but her hands were still shaking and she sliced her left forefinger. She stared at her finger in disbelief, the white line of the cut like thin lips and then the blood welling to run down her finger. She stuck the finger in her mouth and sucked on it, staring out the porthole at the ragged coastline.

In San Alberto Bay, the *Lily Langtry* passed an inbound troller that was rolling so hard her bottom paint showed to the turn of the bilge. After listening to the weather forecast, Buddy opted to anchor in Kelly Cove on the east side of Noyes Island for the night. This would mean a quiet night but a longer run in the morning.

When the engine started at 2:00 a.m. Danny rolled out of his bunk and pulled on his boots. He sat there for a moment, feeling lost and lonely. Nothing quite so desolate as waking in the dead of the night in the fo'c'sle of a fishing boat, no matter that he had done it thousands of times.

He pulled on his jacket and went forward. As the anchor chain came aboard it glittered with some form of bioluminescence, like tiny stars. Danny scraped a bit of mud from the anchor flukes and tossed it overboard to watch the flower of light when it hit the water, an explosion like a nebula in a dark corner of the universe. The *Lily's* bow wave glistened as she got underway, but once out of the cove the light disappeared.

Figuring they would have a rough ride, Danny checked the skiff towline and the safety line that served as backup. He tightened the line that secured the power block to make sure that it would not swing too wildly in the coming waves. Ahead he could see the dark outline of Cone Island against the starlight and fleeing clouds. A boat was transiting the passage in front of the island, showing the faint glow of a running light—red, portside, which meant she was headed inside.

Danny remembered his first summer on the old *Libby 6* when his deckmate Simon had told him a jingle to remember which side of the boat was which—"Tokay okay, port not right." A cheap wine mnemonic. Simon had been dead ten years now, found floating facedown in the Craig harbor one winter morning. Jesus, Danny thought, he had been out here too long.

In the galley, Danny made a pot of coffee and moved the grids on the stovetop to hold the pot in place. He took two mugs forward. Buddy had chosen to take the helm at the steering station by his stateroom, rather than on the flying bridge. In the green light of the radar screen he looked haggard as he stood at the wheel.

Danny sat on the wooden stool lashed to the starboard side. "You want me to watch while you hit the bunk for a bit?" he asked.

Buddy shook his head. "I'm wide awake."

"Gonna earn our pay today," Danny said as spray splattered the wheelhouse windows.

"If there aren't any fish we'll look for a place inside to scratch," Buddy said.

When the *Lily* rounded Cape Addington, the waves were even steeper. Danny went aft to check the skiff, bracing himself against the walls as the companionway rolled and plunged like a funhouse ride. The skiff was humping over the waves, occasionally looking as though it might come aboard the *Lily*'s back deck. The skiff towline would slacken and then come taut with an audible pop. A welter of white foam followed the skiff.

Once the *Lily* cleared the cape and turned north, she took the waves on her stern quarter. Not banging now, but rolling and slewing in the following sea until they crept into the lee of Denise Marlene

Rock. One boat lay at anchor back in the kelp, its galley window a pale square of light. Danny saw it was the *Alaskan*, an old wooden seiner. Her galley light rose and fell against the dark shore.

More than an hour till the 6:00 a.m. opening, Danny went forward to drop the anchor. He let the cable scream out till the drum was down to the last few wraps—extra scope against the weight of the wind.

Back in the galley he shook water from his hair. Toby sat at the table, and Nora was making more coffee.

"Holy mackerel," Toby said. "Ugly out there."

"Just before the battle, mother, the band began to play," Danny said and headed to the fo'c'sle for dry clothing.

At six, the *Alaskan* set her net. Simultaneously the *Viking Hero* set offshore; Sven had elected not to wait in the line. The current was moving back and offshore, and when the *Alaskan* closed her net, she was instantly swept toward the open sea. The *Lily* took her turn and when they began to haul gear the current also took them beyond the loom of land, and they felt the unfettered pressure of the wind. Buddy ran the block slowly, stopping it entirely as the *Lily* rolled to port, then trying to gain a few fathoms of net as she rolled back to starboard. Even so, the net picked Nora right off her feet as it swung wildly. She got back up and soldiered on. When half the seine was aboard, Buddy stopped the block and motioned Nora to come forward.

"You run this," he said, handing her the remote control for the block. "I need a little exercise." He climbed onto the net pile and grabbed the swinging web. "I'm not sure I remember how to do this," he said to Nick with a grin.

They finished the set without incident, and forty fish came aboard in the bag. "Enough of this," Buddy said. "Let's head inside." He climbed to the flying bridge and Nick went aft to hook up the skiff. As he did so the boat rolled so wildly that the entire seine shifted on the sloping deck. The two boats in line behind the *Lily* elected not to set and were now steaming north, but the *Viking Hero*, once it got its gear back, had run inshore and set the net again.

Danny came inside and stripped off his raingear. A yoke of wet from driven rain marked his sweatshirt. "Man!" he said. "Thank God, we're going inside." He peered out through the door's fogged window. "I can't believe Sven set out again."

"For forty fish," Nick grimaced with disbelief.

"Wants everybody to know he's the bull with the big balls."

Toby jumped up and stood beside Danny, looking for the figure in blue on the *Hero*'s back deck.

"There are some boats I just wouldn't work on," Nora said. "Sven and those other assholes would drive me to tears."

"I've never seen Sara cry," Toby said. "I'm not sure anyone has."

Sara stood in the lee of the wheelhouse. She had taken a beating during the first set and was not sure how she was going to make it through the day. The *Alaskan* had finally gotten its gear back and headed inside via Cape Addington. The *Lily* was well north, hull down in the steep waves. Which left the *Viking Hero* alone on the outer coast.

"There goes your boyfriend with the other pussies," Aaron said.

"He's not my—" Sara started to say and then stopped. Just what was Toby to her?

"He'd have been real popular in Walla Walla." Aaron made a grinding motion with his pelvis. Sara closed her eyes and prayed that this, too, would pass. She had to get off this boat before she went mad. She wished Toby was here to deal with Aaron. Toby was so easygoing that people underestimated him, especially if they'd never felt the ropey muscles in his back. He'd been a wrestler or something in high school, one of those things important to guys, and she had seen his Highland eyes flare like heat lightning. Once in Palo Alto they'd run into one of her old boyfriends in a bar. The guy was a bit drunk, and he'd talked down to Toby, who was polite and noncommittal, but when Sara linked her arm with Toby's, it was like grabbing a cable under tension. She said something innocuous and steered Toby toward the door before the other guy's expensive teeth were scattered across the floor like bloody Chiclets. Thinking of it now brought a half grin, her first in days.

When the *Hero* started to haul gear, the wind and tide were so fierce that Aaron could not pull the seine over the block by himself. Sven yelled at Sara to get back there and help him. When she tallied onto the pass rope, Aaron was almost wrapped around her and she nearly vomited at his touch.

The web fought Sara like a wild horse as they stacked gear, and when the bunt came aboard, fewer than twenty fish lay flopping on deck. Without a word, Sven went up to the wheelhouse and headed north.

In the galley, dirty breakfast dishes were piled in the sink, but Sara had no energy to deal with them. She could feel blood trickle down her thigh and a tidal wave of exhaustion swept over her, but at least they were headed inside.

Billy came into the galley and collapsed by the table and almost instantly fell asleep, his mouth gaping open. Twenty minutes later they were opposite Little Roller Bay, and the *Viking Hero* slowed and turned slightly. A wave smashed over the rail and hammered the wheelhouse. Sven shouted down the companionway, "Get ready to set."

Billy snapped awake. "Bastard," he said vehemently, but he gathered his raingear and headed for the skiff.

Oh no, God, no, Sara thought. She grabbed Aaron's arm. "I really need some of those pills," she said with her head down, afraid to meet his eye.

Aaron grinned and took a bottle out of his pocket and spun it on the table, then closed it in his big fist. "Hand job gets you one, blow job gets you two, sweetheart."

"Fuck you," Sara said, but she knew the bravado was empty.

CHAPTER 17

*Shaft Rock, 1.1 miles N. of Cape Addington, is
conical in shape and light brown, and shows
prominently from the S. and N. Known locally
as the Haystack.*

—US Coast Pilot

"In the galley of the *Lily*, Christ was born across the seas. With a glory in his bosom that transfigured you and me," Nick sang as he came in from the back deck.

"Enough with the puns, already," Nora said.

A hard rain drove across Arriaga Passage like an army on the march. The *Lily* was fishing in the lee of St. Joseph Island in a five-boat lineup. Danny put on his rain jacket and headed to the back deck for a cigarette.

"You can smoke inside, Danny," Nora said. "It's just too awful out there."

"Rules is rules," Danny grinned and headed out the door.

Nick looked up, surprised at the underlying tone, shower of sparks when knife touches grindstone.

The rain increased that afternoon but the wind lessened. They made their last set in fading light, then unloaded their few fish to a tender. The deckhands were eating supper when the *Lily* passed Cape Ulitka and began to roll.

"Shit," Nora said and jumped up to secure the galley. She had expected Buddy to anchor in the quiet water behind Cape Ulitka.

"What gives?" Nick asked.

"I dunno," Danny said. "It's laid down quite a bit. We must be gonna anchor outside again."

"But there aren't any fish."

"Maybe Buddy figures this wind will push a slug of fish on shore. He must be hoping for one last kick at the dog."

The *Lily* eased down the coast well offshore, cruising at half speed with her running lights out. Buddy called down for them to douse the galley lights as well. The *Lily* turned toward shore and stopped, riding the swells stern on.

"What's he up to?" Toby asked Danny. The other two had already gone to bed.

"Doesn't want to be the first to anchor up. There's another boat coming, see?"

Toby looked out and saw closer to shore the bright green starboard light of a southbound vessel.

"This time of year, he doesn't want the first set. Days are shorter, fish get moving later. Second or third set's apt to be the hot one."

The *Lily Langtry* was in fact the third boat to anchor in the bight. Early next morning the first boat had a poor set. The second caught a few hundred, but when the *Lily* took her turn, daylight had come and they could see fish jumping in the back of the seine. Buddy closed after twenty minutes. "We got a good one," he said as he came down the ladder.

It proved to be the best set of the year, almost filling the hold. They had to brail slowly in the big rollers that were the aftermath of the storm, and the current took them a long way south. Once the bunt came aboard, Buddy instantly cut Danny loose and set out for the bight full bore, the seine still over the block.

The *Lily* took the inside route, passing between the shore and the skiff of the *Mark Christopher*, the boat that was currently set out. Sitting on the seine pile Toby could see that the *Viking Hero* was also racing for the set, coming down from Little Roller Bay. Buddy curved hard into the bight and then throttled back as the *Viking Hero* boomed in from the north.

Danny caught up with the *Lily*, and as they hooked up the skiff release, the *Hero* came alongside. Sven came out and leaned on the rail. "It's my set," he announced.

Buddy paid him no mind but simply sat at the wheel, watching the *Mark Christopher*.

"I'm takin' it," Sven said and went back in the wheelhouse, then turned and came back out. "You tell Milo I'm gonna buy that fuckin' boat and sink it, just to get it out of my way."

"It's not their set, is it?" Nick asked Danny as the skiff man came aboard.

"No fuckin' way. It wasn't even close."

"Then what's Sven up to?"

"Rattlin' Buddy's cage, like the other day. Trying to steal a set. But Buddy wants this one, and he'll call Sven's bluff."

Only it wasn't a bluff. Buddy moved into position as the *Mark Christopher* closed her net. The *Viking Hero* edged closer but then turned away. Toby pulled the skiff release and Danny gunned the skiff engine as he turned to begin the tow. Almost instantly Sven put the *Viking Hero's* rudder hard over and raced back toward them, then swerved and released her skiff when little more than ten fathoms away. The *Hero* flashed by, setting the net at a tremendous rate. Sven leaned out the wheelhouse window and looked at them stonily. In the *Hero's* skiff Billy stood on the bench seat and bent over, pointing his backside at them and rubbing it suggestively.

Nick and Toby exchanged disgusted glances. "Sonsabitches," Nick said. But then the *Lily* slowed. They had less than thirty fathoms of gear in the water, and Buddy brought the *Lily* almost to a halt and then turned back toward shore, the seine slipping off the stern ever more slowly as Buddy curved in a switchback. The *Lily* walked a tightrope between its own cork line and the *Hero's*. When Buddy gained enough room he turned the corner and cut inside the *Hero's* skiff. He began to tow out, but now the *Lily* was in front of the *Viking Hero's* net, rather than behind.

Toby let out a whoop and looked up at the bridge, wishing he could high-five Buddy who was watching the net impassively. In the *Hero's* skiff Billy sat dumbfounded, his mouth hanging open while Danny towed hard to keep his end of the *Lily's* seine clear. As he passed

Billy's skiff Danny put his right hand inside his left elbow and jerked his left arm up in the classic "fuck you" gesture.

Buddy ran the net out scarcely two fathoms in front of Sven's seine, cork for cork. When the seine was fully set, he put a sort of insouciant hook in the end, all without so much as looking at the *Viking Hero*. He had not left the *Hero* enough room to close up, and Sven had to tow offshore to gain sufficient space to work the gear. Toby looked across the water. Sara was slumped against the wheelhouse, one sleeve of her rain jacket on, one off. She looked as though she had no idea where she was.

For all that trouble, when the *Lily* hauled back she had no more than five hundred fish, but Danny came aboard laughing. "Fuck me to tears," he said. "That was the funniest thing I ever saw. Buddy left Sven with his ass hanging out. Guys are already laughing about it on the radio."

"Was it Billy's fault?"

"Hell, no. Sven just left Buddy too much room. Tell you the truth I didn't think Buddy could pull it off—too tight. But Sven'll have to blame somebody. He'll cut Billy a new asshole. And everybody else on that boat."

Sara was not sure exactly what had happened. They had set in front of the *Lily Langtry*, and the next thing she knew the *Lily* was in front of them. Sven came out of the wheelhouse and screamed profanities so loudly that Billy must have heard them in the skiff 250 fathoms away. They towed offshore, closed up, and began to haul gear. Sven ran the block at a merciless speed, not even slowing down when the bunt came aboard without any fish, ripping the last of the net up and through the block without the pass rope so that it fell heavily, almost knocking Sara off her feet.

Sven climbed to the bridge and headed north, scarcely allowing time to hook up the skiff. Before they reached Little Roller Bay he set the net again, so close to the boats back at the Haystack that he was practically cutting them off. He held the net open a very short time and again hauled the gear at breakneck speed, trying to bury the crew.

Tempers frayed on deck. Aaron and Scott cursed Sven, Billy, each other. Sara was so near collapse that she began to think no price was too great to end this torment. They moved north to Little Roller and set again. This time they towed around a flock of rhinoceros auklets feeding in a rip. As the cork line drew tight like a noose, the auklets huddled up, disconcerted. A few took long scuttering runs across the water and managed to clamber across the corks. One bird dove and became caught in the web. As the power block ripped the cork line from the water the bird was borne skyward, dangling from one wing.

"Bird," Sara yelled. Usually they stopped the block to free any tangled bird, but this time Sven did not even slow down as the bird came over the block. Sara thought the auklet gave her a beseeching look as it fell. "Bird," she yelled again and made a desperate grab for it, going down on her hands and knees on the pile. But Sven did not stop the block, and the web fell on top of Sara, entangling her. She scrabbled through the web, searching for the auklet. Somehow her whole summer was wrapped in the bird, as though saving it would save her soul, but it disappeared into the pile, and Sara struggled against the cloud of web till it buried her as well.

Finally, Sven stopped the block and Sara rolled free. Shaking her hood back she scrambled across the pile and stood on deck glaring at Sven, both of her blue arms extended and orange-gloved hands raised with middle fingers extended. "You son of a bitch," she screamed.

"Back on the pile," Sven said contemptuously, gesturing with his left hand, the right still holding the remote control.

"Back up, I want to save that bird." Sara moved toward him, so angry she was shaking.

"Get back on the fucking pile."

Sara kicked him in the shins and Sven lashed out with a left-hand punch that caught her right eye and sent her flying backward.

She almost blacked out for a moment, spinning as she fell on the slippery deck. Her nose cracked against one of the deck dividers and she ended up sitting on the deck, her legs sprawled in front of her like a ragdoll. She clutched her eye in disbelief; blood slid down the back of her throat from her nose. Aaron stared at her impassively. Scott had a silly grin; he looked at Aaron, trying to imitate the big boys.

Then Sara heard the roar of the skiff and felt it slam into the side of the *Hero*. Billy jumped over the rail screaming, "You asshole!" He ran at Sven full tilt, but Sven straight-armed him, knocking him down. Undaunted, Billy jumped up and tackled Sven. The two rolled on the deck, a multicolor tangle of raingear till Aaron came down from the pile and pulled Billy off Sven, pinioning his arms.

For one murderous moment Sven looked as though he was going to smash Billy full in the face; instead he picked up the remote control and heaved it at the wheelhouse. It bounced off, tethered by its cord. Sven drew a deep breath, looked at Sara, and then out to sea.

"All right," he said. "Let's get the net back, head for Petersburg. There aren't any fish anyhow."

He went into the galley and brought Sara a length of paper towel. She was still sitting wordlessly on deck, blood streaking her raingear. During the melee, Scott, of all people, had the presence of mind to grab the skiff painter with a boat hook and tie it to the davit. Billy climbed back into the skiff, his manner an odd combination of swagger and offended dignity—the aggrieved gunslinger. Sara stuffed some paper towel in her nose and climbed back on the net pile. She looked dully at the mound of web. No doubt the auklet was dead. During the interruption, the net had drifted around the stern and the other birds had all escaped.

They hauled gear slowly, and six fish came aboard—five humpies and a coho. Sven climbed to the flying bridge without a backward glance. While the boys lifted and chained the skiff, Sara stood at the kitchen sink trying to scrub clean. She heard Sven come down the companionway and stand behind her, but she did not turn around.

Sven cleared his throat and said, "I'm sorry, Sara. I lost my temper. It's been a hard year. The wife . . ." His voice trailed off.

Sara turned around, wanting him to see the blood and the blackened eye. "I want you to take me to the *Lily Langtry*."

"I can't do that," Sven said, not that boat of all boats.

"Then one of the tenders at Cape Ulitka."

"They won't be going in till late tonight. You'll get there faster with us."

"I don't want to spend one more minute on this boat. Not one fucking minute."

"Suit yourself," Sven said coldly and turned away, as though Sara's anger had exculpated his own.

Sara wadded up her raingear and carried it to the fo'c'sle. She began to pull clothing from her locker and stuff it in her rucksack. Bending over made her eye throb painfully. Her back was turned to the galley and she had a sudden, intense vision of Aaron pinning her against her bunk. She spun around but there was no one there. She sat down on the bunk with her head in her hands. She would never let them see her cry.

CHAPTER 18

Wrangell Narrows is marked by an extensive
system of lights, lighted ranges, daybeacons,
and buoys. . . . It is safest to enter either end
late on a flood tide.

—*US Coast Pilot*

The morning fog began to lift as the *Lily Langtry* reached the maze of markers by Blind Slough, at the outskirts of Petersburg. A cutter was moored at the Coast Guard dock, the orange slash on its side a blazon in the autumnal mix of mist and light.

Seeing the cutter made Nora realize that she had not thought of Melody for more than a week. The memory was fading, like a traveler's voice growing fainter with distance.

The *Lily* went directly to the pumps. Nora hurried to the pay phone by the cannery office, anxious to call her daughter. Luckily Trish answered after the first ring.

"Hi, sweetie," Nora said.

"Oh, hi, Mom."

"How are you doing?"

"Well, for starters, I kicked Duane out."

"Good riddance."

"I guess."

"Did he take your car?" Nora asked, though it was the last thing she cared about.

"He tried to. Said it was half his because of all the work he did on it. About all he ever did was change the oil, the jerk."

Trish said something else, but it was drowned by the sound of a passing forklift. Nora waited for a moment, trying to think how to phrase the important question, fearful of the perpetually thin ice of mother-daughter relationships.

"Did you take the test?" she asked, finally.

"Yes I did and I am pregnant," Trish said matter-of-factly.

"Oh dear, oh dear. You're a nurse, you should have known better," Nora blurted out.

"Mom, it's okay. You raised me alone, and I came out all right, didn't I?"

"Oh, sweetheart," Nora said. Trish had no idea of the pain, the loneliness, the despair.

"Look, Mom, I gotta go. I'm late for work already," Trish said and hung up.

Nora knew she should have been more sympathetic, but the news was too upsetting. She needed order and sanity, and she gathered her laundry and headed for the apartment. Unlocking the door was like entering another world. After so many weeks on the boat the cleanliness and the quiet—the sense of a dry, stable space—was unimaginably luxurious. She opened the windows to freshen the air. In a juniper bush in the garden she could see a Steller's jay, bright blue back and black head and tail.

A quick knock and Danny Sullivan appeared at her door. "We got a problem," he said abruptly. "I ran into Billy Nichols. He just quit Sven's boat. Apparently Sven beat up Sara pretty bad, and Billy walked off."

"Beat up Sara? Oh my God. Where is she?"

"She's coming in on the *Vera Lynn*. The cannery told me she'd be here pretty soon. They just called from Scow Bay."

"Does Toby know?"

"Not yet. I thought I should let you know first."

"Sweet suffering Jesus," Nora said, pulling on her shoes. "The poor child. I better go get her. We've gotta keep Toby away from her. He'll stick his foot in it, I know he will."

Nora hurried out the door and down the sidewalk. Danny could barely keep up with her. "What exactly happened?" she asked.

"I don't really know. Sven was sore about something, and she talked back to him, and he popped her."

"Jesus Lord."

"Billy said he jumped Sven and was beating the shit out of him, but the others pulled him off."

"Billy?" Nora almost stopped in her tracks. "Beating up Sven?"

"Well . . . Billy'd already been drinking when he told me the story. So how much we should believe . . ."

"Where's Toby?"

"He went for a run. I expect he'll shower at the cannery when he gets back."

"Just keep him away."

Nora found the *Vera Lynn* tied outside the *Muskrat* at the cold storage dock. As she walked toward it, Sara Quan slung her rucksack and duffel bag onto the dock and turned to wave goodbye. When she turned back Nora could see she had a textbook shiner.

"Oh, hi," she said to Nora and touched her hand to her black eye. "I guess you heard."

"Danny Sullivan told me. Do you need a place to stay?"

"I was thinking of getting a hotel room. I've got a plane ticket tomorrow, and I could probably crash at the dorm, but I don't want all the questions."

"Come stay with me." Nora picked up the duffel bag to seal the arrangement. "You can take a nice, long bath."

"A bath, wow, what a concept."

As they walked through the cold storage, Sara kept her head down so that her hair partly shielded her face, but her eyes darted from side to side. "Is Toby around?" she asked.

"Somewhere."

"I'd just as soon not have to talk to him."

"I told Danny to keep him away."

They climbed the hill toward the apartment. Sara sighed. "So ends the big Alaskan adventure. Now I've got to figure what to tell them at home. Showing up reeking of fish and diesel and with a black eye."

"The smell will fade. So will the black eye."

Sara shot a quick glance at Nora, as if to gauge whether her knowledge of black eyes was firsthand. Nora was, in fact, thinking of the first black eye Buck had given her. Some meaningless argument while they were drinking Jack Daniels. Buck had taken a swing at her, probably just a feint, but he was so drunk that the punch had gone awry, and she was so drunk that she had dodged the wrong way and got knocked off the kitchen chair, waking the baby. Afterward Buck had been sickeningly apologetic for about three days, and then somehow it all became her fault. She shuddered at the memory, not of the black eye, but of the marriage and of the logging camp—the raw slash of the clear-cuts and the gaggle of trailers rusting beneath the endless rain.

Sara wanted a cup of tea before her bath. Nora made a pot and brought it to the table. "Thank you," Sara said calmly. She had taken off her jacket. Beneath she was wearing a Silver Lining Seafood T-shirt that showed her slender brown arms and the simple gold chain around her throat. Nora felt a twinge of resentment. Sara was too composed, too elegant; the black eye almost looked as though it had been done with mascara.

"What actually happened?" Nora asked.

"Not that much. Sven was being a jerk, and I flipped him off, and he took a swing at me."

"Did Billy Nichols really try to save you?"

"Go figure. Of all the people to play Lochinvar," Sara laughed, but then she looked out the window. "Oh, shit, here comes Toby."

"It's all right, you don't look that bad."

"It's not that. I just really, really don't want to hear 'I told you so.'"

Nora stepped out the door and closed it firmly behind her.

"How is she?" Toby asked, trying to look around Nora.

"Taking a bath," Nora lied. "She's not ready to talk to anybody. Including you."

"Why not?"

"I don't know. Would you want to talk about it?"

"Sara," Toby sighed, a kaleidoscope of emotions in the single word. Obviously, he did not understand the situation. Neither did Nora. There was something off-kilter about Sara's reaction, and Nora was beginning to regret her initial sympathy. What was the big deal if some yuppie princess got popped in her flawless snoot?

"Look, you really want to help?" she asked Toby.

"Sure. Of course."

"Mow the lawn." Nora slipped back inside and turned the deadbolt.

"Thank you," Sara said.

"I'll run the bathwater for you," Nora said and turned away.

Sara heard the water cascade into the tub. She looked around the sunlit kitchen, listened to the whir of the mower beyond the window. She was grateful for the normalcy, for the blue teapot and the fragrant tea in a thin china teacup. She briefly considered telling Nora about Aaron, but that was one memory she wanted to bury so deeply that it would never again reach the light of day.

"All ready," Nora said. "Hot water, bubble bath, fluffy towels."

"A maiden's prayer," Sara said. She raised the teacup to her lips for a last sip. She remembered her grandmother endlessly drinking green tea in tiny porcelain cups. But then she felt Aaron's rough hands on her body, familiar and contemptuous. Her own hands began to tremble violently. She tried to put the cup back on the saucer she held in her left hand, but the rattling noise startled her and she dropped them both. The cup broke when it hit the table, the last of the tea splattering across the Formica.

"Oh, shit. Oh, shit," Sara said, drawing a deep, sobbing breath. "I'm sorry. I'm sorry." She tried to quell the sobs but they racked her body from deep within till she shook like a blade of grass in a gale, tears streaming down her face. "I'm just so sorry."

"Never you mind, honey," Nora said and put her arms around Sara and rocked her gently. "Just never you mind."

Once Sara was in the bathtub Nora went outside and sat on the stoop and leaned back against the closed door. The Steller's jay chattered loudly from the juniper bush, beautiful plumage but noisy and troublesome, like most of the humans Nora knew.

Toby and Nick were raking. Nick had showed up and without a comment or a question had started to help. Nora recognized the quiet support as a typical Nick gesture. Unless he was there to cadge a meal, which would be equally typical. Nick could be so exasperatingly male, with the cigars and the wisecracks, and then he would show a sensitivity that was almost feminine. Nora could not figure him out, but this was her summer to understand not much of anything.

After her bath Sara wanted to lie down. Nora thought a little solitude would be the best thing for Sara, and she decided to walk to the harbor with Nick and check the *Guinevere*. Toby took off for a walk in the opposite direction, still visibly upset. Before he left, Nora pointedly locked the door and made him promise not to double back and bother Sara. He could call later, maybe she would want to see him.

The *Guinevere* was cold and damp and musty. Nick started the oil stove while Nora rummaged beneath the sink for cleaning supplies. She began to scour the counters and woodwork, suddenly angry at the world of men and boats.

"You don't have to do that," Nick said.

"Yes, I do."

"Is it part of the genetic code or something?"

"Not linked to the Y chromosome, anyway." Nora opened the cupboards and began to throw out the mildewed boxes. Cleaning the boat the way General Sherman had tidied Georgia.

Finally, her anger abated, she sat with Nick on the rail, sharing a last beer he had found. The *Viking Hero* was moored to a nearby finger float, no one visible onboard. A small boy wearing a Seattle Mariners cap was jigging for herring from the dock, using a setup of small gold hooks that were devoid of bait. As they watched, the boy caught a fat herring with iridescent green-gold scales and put it in a five-gallon bucket.

"So how's Sara?" Nick asked.

"Okay, I guess. At first she was a little flippant, but deep down she's hurting. I don't think we're getting the whole story. I'd really like to know what's going on."

"What do you mean?"

"On the *Viking Hero*. Too many weird things happening."

"Like Danny says, it's a bad luck boat."

"What kind of explanation is that?"

"Uh-oh," Nick said. Toby was coming down the ramp, head bent in his shambling, professorial walk, while Sven Oslund had just climbed over the rail of the *Viking Hero* and started their way.

Nora had a moment's irrational hope that Toby would not even notice Sven, but Toby suddenly stiffened and moved into Sven's path, stopping him. Nora heard angry voices and then Sven tried to shove Toby out of the way, but Toby gave no ground. He widened his stance and held his hands up, palms open. From the corner of her eye, Nora saw Nick grab a weighted gaff hook and put his foot on the rail. Toby feinted at Sven who took a roundhouse swing. Toby sidestepped and came in at an angle and jammed Sven in the chin with an open palm, forcing him back. Sven lifted a foot to keep balance and Toby reached down and grabbed the uplifted ankle and neatly levered Sven backward into the water.

"Boy, howdy," Nick said as Sven hit the water with a resounding splash. The kid in the Mariners cap stood transfixed, his mouth open, his fishing rod lifted. A bright silver herring dangled in midair, twisted free, and was gone.

CHAPTER 19

*Scow Bay, on the E side of Wrangell Narrows
is about 2 miles below Petersburg and immediately
S of Blunt Point. At night, the lights from the
community of Scow Bay show prominently on the Narrows.*
—US Coast Pilot

"Hey, white man, come up and drink with me."

"Hey, Danny." Toby lay on his bunk, hands clasped behind his head, thinking about Sara, thinking about school, thinking about the birth of tragedy and the genealogy of morals.

"C'mon, man, I gotta buy you a drink. You're a fucking celebratory. People been wanting to toss Sven in the drink for years."

"Happy to oblige." Toby stood up, yawning. "I gotta call Sara, see if I can stop by."

"She'll keep. You can call her from the bar."

Kito's Kave—dim lights, a jukebox, crowded tables. Billy Nichols sat at the bar with a pile of crumpled bills and change in front of him. He looked as though he had moved in to stay. He waved them over and stuck out his hand for a high-five.

"Hey, kid," he said. "I heard what you done. I was gonna throw him over the side myself."

"Good tag team," Danny said with a broad wink to Toby as they sat down. "So what's Sven gonna do for a crew now?"

"Aaron said Sven's gonna put the drum on, go longlining. There's a black cod opener in Chatham Strait in ten days."

"How about you?" Danny asked as he signaled for three beers.

"I'm outa here. There's a ferry at 4:00 a.m. I'm gonna head south, maybe fish Puget Sound."

"Nice, easy duty. Plus you spend your nights in Ballard instead of Petersburg."

"Fuckin' babes everywhere."

"Speaking of which," Toby said. He walked over to the pay phones and called Nora. When she answered, he asked if he could come see Sara or at least talk to her. Nora hesitated a moment and then said, "She's already in bed. I don't want to disturb her."

"Oh . . ." Toby said. Was it too much to ask for? A moment of talk with Sara, some acknowledgment that he was allowed to be concerned?

"She said you could stop by in the morning before her plane."

"Yeah, okay, maybe."

When Toby got back to his barstool, Billy said, "Your girlfriend, she's a class act. I don't know where Sven got off, treating her like trailer trash. You can't smack a lady."

"Nope," Toby said. Did this mean Billy thought it was permissible to hit women who live in mobile homes?

"The books she reads, the stuff she cooks. A real highliner. Nice ass too." Billy put a companionable arm around Toby's shoulders. He smelled as though he had been baptized in bourbon. Full immersion.

"Look, you're a fisherman," Billy said. "You gotta have a waterfall. Hey, Donna, three waterfalls."

The barmaid was a middle-aged woman with breasts like wine bladders. She was wearing a T-shirt that said, "When Lutefisk is Outlawed Only Outlaws Will Have Lutefisk." She set two shot glasses in front of each of the boys. She filled three with tequila, three with schnapps.

"Show him, Danny," Billy said.

"It's like this." Danny held one glass between the forefinger and middle finger of his right hand, the other between the middle finger and ring finger. "You gotta toss 'em all at once." He nodded to Toby and tilted his head back and drained the glasses. "Waterfall," he said in a rasping voice.

Toby followed suit. A splash of drowning at the back of his throat, a path of fire burning up his nostrils. "Wow," he said. "That certainly clears the sinuses." He grabbed his beer and took a long swig.

"College girls," Billy said as he signaled for another round. "I just don't get it. You go in a bar in Ballard and start hustlin' chicks, and it's like you both know the rules. College girls, it's a whole 'nother game. Sara, she made me kinda uneasy, you wanna know the truth."

"Sara likes to keep guys off balance. She's good at it." Toby said.

"I couldn't figure Aaron sniffin' after her. Good way to get in trouble, messing with somebody like that. So what if she's a tasty piece." Billy nodded knowingly.

"Aaron?" Toby said.

"Donna, hey, barkeep," Danny interrupted. "A round of prairie fires if you please."

"Prairie fire? That's a new one," Donna said.

"It's a shot of tequila with four drops of Tabasco."

"Good eye opener," Donna said and mixed the drinks.

Toby knocked his back. The tequila blurred; the pepper clarified. His turn to buy, he signaled for more prairie fires. The walls and ceiling now met at something other than right angles. Everyone looked vaguely familiar, and the jukebox played songs he almost knew.

"Aaron going black codding with Sven?" Danny asked Billy.

"I dunno. He said he's about had enough."

"Fed up with Sven?"

"Yeah, plus he figures a bust's comin' down. Too much loose talk." Billy held an admonishing finger to his lips to signal silence.

"Oh, fuck," Danny said and looked around the bar.

"I got half a mind to rat Sven out myself, the bastard. I could send him away for a long time." Billy nodded sagely.

Toby stumbled to the bathroom and leaned into the urinal. A Rainier poster showed a girl with remarkable jugs. Lewd messages were scrawled on the walls and he remembered finding Sara's name written on the men's room wall of a pizza joint in Palo Alto.

When he returned, Aaron had materialized on the stool next to Billy. Where had he come from?

"Let's go to the Homestead," Billy said. "I need some ham and eggs. I can drink coffee till the ferry."

"Bad idea." Danny took hold of one of Billy's arms, Aaron took the other. "We'd get popped for public drunkenness or some shit. Let's go out to my place, eat some chili."

In Sing Lee Alley was a Ford Fairlane with rusted rocker panels, Aaron behind the wheel. Toby was not quite sure how or why he was part of this, but he got in the back seat with Billy. Overhead a fishy bit of moon trolled the night sky.

Danny's place was a one-room shack on pilings by the edge of Scow Bay. Toby collapsed onto an easy chair with broken springs, so drunk his attention fixed on small items—gray mold on an open can of bean dip, a dusty mousetrap clasping a long-dead mouse.

Danny lit the propane cook stove and dumped two cans of chili in a saucepan. From a shelf he took garlic powder and a bottle of Mongolian Fire Oil. "Bering Sea chili," Danny said. "Specialty de la maison. Excuse my fucking French."

Aaron produced a bottle of Jose Cuervo and broke the seal. He poured Billy a water glass full. "Drink up, partner," he said.

"That prick Sven, I could cause him big trouble." Billy drank off half the glass. "Did I tell you him and Melody had a fight the night she went over? A screamin', fuckin' catfight. I was on watch, but I could hear it, even over the main."

"That's one can of worms you most definitely do not want to open." Danny tasted the chili judiciously. "Needs diesel," he said.

"You got any papers?" Aaron asked as he pulled a plastic baggie from his jacket pocket. "Fuck it," he said. "I'll just make a bong." He took an empty Rainier can from an overflowing trash can, crumpled it in the middle, and worked it till there was a slight tear. He put a pinch of grass on the can, lit it with a kitchen match, and then inhaled through the keyhole tab opening.

"Urban survival skills," said Danny.

"I'm a fuckin' Daniel Boone of the streets." Aaron passed the beer can to Toby who dropped it. He jumped up and brushed the embers off.

Aaron retrieved the bong, put another pinch in it, lit it and took a hit, then passed it to Toby. "Here, college boy, see if you can keep from pissin' on yourself."

Toby felt his fists clench involuntarily, but it was as though he was trying to grab water.

"Hey, back off, you guys," Danny said. "Chili's ready." He handed 'round four mismatched bowls.

The chili burned Toby's mouth. Danny gave him a beer and poured another glass full of tequila for Billy.

"Fuckin' Sven, I'm gonna take him down," Billy said. "Where's your phone?"

"There ain't any," Danny said. "Forget about it. We're gonna put you on the ferry if we have to pour you on."

Aaron lit the bong again. His gaze fastened on Billy. He shook out the match.

CHAPTER 20

Ratz Harbor, about 7 miles NNW of Narrow
Point, is a small anchorage that is little more
than 0.5 mile long and 0.2 mile wide. . . . Williwaws
from the SE at times strike with great force
in this anchorage.

—US Coast Pilot

Toby awoke in the chair. Danny and Billy and Aaron were gone. He stumbled out to the back deck and relieved himself, watching two seiners headed down the Narrows. Oh, no, he thought, we're fishing tomorrow. Back inside, he stood at the kitchen tap and gulped down water. His saliva tasted like fish slime.

He closed the front door behind him, put the padlock on the hasp, and began to walk north, a light rain falling. At the outskirts of town, he heard the distant roar of a jet. He saw it clear the trees and turn south, still climbing. No doubt Sara was onboard, bound for a different world. Did it matter that he had not said goodbye?

An ambulance was parked by the ferry terminal alongside two police cars. A few onlookers stood in a knot, but Toby did not stop. In the harbor, he found the *Lily* tied to the outermost float, her engine running. Danny was asleep in the fo'c'sle, and Buddy sat at the galley table studying a chart of Etolin Island. The run on the outer coast was over, Buddy had told the crew. It was time to move inside. He planned to fish District 6, south of Petersburg.

Nick and Nora appeared, carrying bags of groceries. "Time to blow this pop stand," Nick said with a grin. He studied Toby's red-rimmed eyes, matted hair, rumpled clothes. "Jesus, kid, you look more like a fisherman every day."

Toby took the first watch, up on the flying bridge, gulping the fresh air. The rain had stopped and a flock of phalaropes worked a tide rip.

He looked for the tin roof of Danny's shack as they transited Scow Bay. What exactly had happened there?

Nora appeared with a mug of coffee and two aspirin for him. "I'm sorry I missed Sara," Toby said. "I feel like such an idiot. I guess I'll have to call her when we get back."

"Maybe it's just as well. She still wasn't herself." That morning Sara had been distracted and edgy, veering from melancholy to brittle speech. Nora had felt relieved when the taxi arrived to take Sara to the airport, but then Sara had given her a heartfelt hug, tears misting her eyes, which left Nora more confused than ever.

Nora looked at Toby—watch cap pulled low over his forehead, nose like a beak, big hands on the steering wheel—not exactly what she would expect Sara Quan to choose. On the other hand, she could certainly understand why any man would find Sara seductive and perhaps the flip side of that coin was that any woman, even Sara, would find Toby's lack of guile and easy demeanor endearing. She patted him on the shoulder and went below.

"Did you hear the news?" Nick said to her. "Some guy on the VHF said Billy Nichols was found dead in the bushes by the ferry terminal."

"Billy, dead? How?"

"Rumor is he choked on his own vomit. Or acute alcohol poisoning."

"Oh my God." Nora had not seen much to like in Billy, but still, he was human. Somewhere, sometime, someone must have cared for him. And would now mourn him.

They fished Etolin Island in the first of the fall rains: Steamer Point at high water, then down to Lincoln Rock. The second day they crossed to Ratz Harbor. Toby had expected fishing inside waters to be easier, but the days were just as long and the jellyfish in the wind stung as badly.

Danny sat alone in the skiff, huddled against the cold. The galley windows were misted over. It would be warm in there, with fresh coffee, but Danny did not want to face Nora's questions. He liked this crew, liked the way they worked together. If he ever ran his own boat Nick and Toby would be his first choice for crew, no matter their lack of experience. He even admired Nora for her toughness and independence. He wished that he had hooked up with this bunch years ago, but it was too late; any chance for redemption was already gone way downstream.

The galley door opened, and Nora came out carrying a lunch basket. Shit, Danny thought; usually she had Toby bring his lunch back. Nora climbed across the seine pile and boarded the skiff. Danny opened the lunch—thermos of coffee, thermos of soup, a couple of hot sandwiches. No one could complain about that, but his stomach tightened under Nora's unwavering gaze.

"What happened, Danny?"

"Whaddaya mean?"

"You know."

"Ask Toby, he was there."

"He said he was passed out."

"So was I. I helped Aaron get Billy in the car, and the next thing I know I'm waking up in the back seat in the harbor parking lot."

"Danny—"

"We were all completely fucked up, you wanna know."

"Danny, two people have died on the *Viking Hero*. What's going on?"

"So you think Aaron stuck his finger down Billy's throat till he puked? Billy was a binge drinker; everybody knew it. And Melody, Christ, she was so far gone it's a wonder she lasted as long as she did."

"It doesn't add up. Somebody's got to talk to the cops."

"Me? Talk to the cops? Are you crazy?"

A burst of smoke came from the *Lily*'s stack as she moved into position to set. Toby and Nick came out on deck. Nora gave Danny a last, hard look and climbed back over the stern of the big boat.

When Nick pulled the skiff release, Danny cranked the wheel hard over and opened the throttle. He thought about what Aaron and Mano would do to someone who ratted them out. His stomach moved as though he'd swallowed a wolf eel.

CHAPTER 21

Wrangell is a city on the N side of Wrangell
Harbor, 89 miles from Ketchikan and 148
miles from Juneau. . . . The approach to Wrangell
Harbor is clear of danger.

—US Coast Pilot

"Pretty ballsy move." Danny looked over the stern of the boat. The screw tossed up plumes of sand. Not far away they could see the exposed sandbars of the Stikine River flats.

In Petersburg, after they left Ratz Harbor, Danny and Toby had talked with the police about their night with Billy. They were unable to add anything to what Aaron had already told them. Billy's blood alcohol had been more than four times the legal limit for driving, possibly lethal.

The interview took time, and when the *Lily* left town Buddy elected to go east down the backside of Mitkof Island rather than through the Narrows. They were headed to Earl West Cove on the east side of Wrangell Island and this route was a considerable shortcut.

"How come there aren't any channel markers?" Toby asked.

"Wouldn't do any good, the river moves around too much. Guys used to go this way in smaller boats, but I don't know of a seiner that's done it in years. Buddy, he's not afraid to take chances."

Earl West was a hatchery release sight. King salmon fingerlings were held in pens there for a short time and then released. When the fish matured, their homing instinct brought them back to Earl West, where no spawning beds awaited, only fish nets.

The next morning only two other boats were in the cove, their white hulls reflected in water so calm that it looked a polished, lustrous green beneath the fog.

On the *Lily's* first set three king salmon, big fish with the coppery color of spawners, came aboard in the bunt. They set again, and this time not a single fish came over the rail—a water haul.

"Sorry, guys," Buddy said. "I just wanted to see what this place was all about. Let's head in to Wrangell. No point going to the cannery, we'll find somebody to give these fish to."

The sun was up now, a beautiful, early fall day. Toby watched an eight-point Sitka blacktail deer swim the back channel.

"If Wrangell is the *Lily's* home port how come we deliver to Petersburg?" he asked Danny.

"Wrangell is more of a logging town, used to be two mills running. There's a small cannery, but it doesn't have much of a tender fleet. You wanna fish the outer coast, it's best to deal with Petersburg. Most of the good fishermen end up there."

When they doubled the point at the north end of Wrangell Island, Nora saw the roofs of her hometown for the first time in twenty years. The sawmill was closed now. Its office and the building that housed the head rig were still standing, but gone were the stacks of cut lumber and gone the big Buddha-shaped scrap burner that glowed in her childhood nights like a gigantic jack-o'-lantern. Nora remembered her father sitting at the supper table in his undershirt and suspenders, home from the mill.

After the *Lily* tied up, Nora walked uptown alone. Not exactly a triumphant return, limping into town on an old seiner with three fish in the hold. Nora scanned the passersby, looking for familiar faces but perversely wishing she was invisible. Now that the mill had closed, the town looked run-down. Potholes pockmarked the street and moss shingled the roofs of the small houses. The old Salvation Army church on Front Street had burned to the ground, gone was its white clapboard steeple, replaced by weeds.

There was one new business, however. A café was about to open in a building that had once held a sporting goods store. Through the window Nora could see the bustle of last-minute preparations. Packing cartons were open on the floor and an electrician stood on a ladder wiring light fixtures. Nora recognized him as one of the neighborhood kids. His ball cap had fallen off to reveal a fringed bald spot.

"Milly's Café" said the sign on the window. Milly, thought Nora. She opened the door and stepped inside. A middle-aged woman with a harried expression looked up and stepped her way as though to tell her they were not open. But then she stopped and said, "Nora?"

In the next five minutes Nora learned that her childhood best friend had started a business with the settlement from her husband's death in a logging accident.

"Supposed to open next week," Milly said. "Brilliant, huh? The whole town's on the skids and I open a café."

"Even the unemployed gotta drink coffee," Nora said, though she agreed it was quite a gamble to open a café in a dying mill town. However, by the end of their conversation, Nora had accepted Milly's offer of a winter job.

That evening she was afraid to tell Buddy of her sudden change of plans, but he took the news with a grin and said there would be a place for her on the boat the following season if she wanted.

The next day Nora began to look for an apartment to rent. When she returned to the harbor in the afternoon, she saw that a boat she used to know, the *Copper King*, was on the timber-framed grid near the old Reliance cannery. Two crewman in hip boots scrubbed her wooden hull. Rust weeped from the fastenings.

Buddy Stepovich leaned against the dock railing watching the men. Despite the chill air he wore a Hawaiian shirt with a bright, floral pattern. He was sucking on a red lollipop.

"Not too many years left in the old hulk," he said as Nora approached.

"You mean the *Copper King* or us?"

"Both." Buddy threw the lollipop stick into the water. Below them an abandoned beam trawl was clad with barnacles.

Nora looked at Buddy. His bright shirt, tweed cap, and wool trousers showed a trace of the old jaunty style. After a summer of living in close quarters, Nora had no more insight into his soul than when they were young.

"Milo listed the *Lily* with a broker," Buddy said suddenly.

"Are you going to make an offer?"

"I gotta talk to the bank."

"He wouldn't sell it out from under you, would he?" she asked.

"Make Milo the right offer, he'd sell the boat, Mom, me. His own soul if he still had it."

"What's your mother think?"

"They had a screaming fight this morning. Mom throwing pots and pans. I had to leave the house." Buddy grinned.

"About the *Lily?*"

"Nope. The *Wrangell Sentinel* came out today and they have this column, what happened in Wrangell five years ago, ten years, you know?"

"Yeah."

"Well, forty years ago this week the old man sunk the *Ranger* up in Icy Strait. Had a full load of dog salmon on board, too."

"And that made your mom mad?"

"Well, the paper listed the survivors, and Milo had this woman along as cook, Eva Ste. Germaine."

"I remember her. Worked as a barmaid, always wore a lot of makeup?"

"Yeah. No doubt she and Milo had a thing going on the side. And Mom, she could purely not abide to see Eva's name in print alongside Milo's, even after forty years. I thought she was going to brain him with his walker."

Buddy unwrapped another lollipop, lemon this time. "First trip I ever made with the old man."

"You were on board?" Nora thought it a little strange to take your young son and your floozie on the same crew. But that was Milo—arrogant, selfish, manipulative.

"I was in the fo'c'sle, asleep, when she rolled over. The old man pulled me out through the forward hatch, I don't know how. If she'd rolled the other way I wouldn't be here."

Three weeks later Nick stood on the bridge where Ketchikan Creek reached tidewater. Yellow devil's club leaves carpeted the bottom of the pool and a few spawned-out salmon wavered in the current. The fish were twisted and dark, with calico patterns of mold across their backs, but still they faced upstream as if trying to understand the long circle of departure and return they had just completed.

Since leaving Wrangell, the *Lily Langtry* had fished for dog salmon up north in Excursion Inlet and then all the way south to Nakat Bay, below Ketchikan. The boat was less of a home without Nora. Buddy had hired an out-of-work millhand named Boyd to take her place, and the galley was again filled with cigarette smoke and the smell of fried food. Buddy's stomach was bothering him, and he spent his free time in his bunk. Toby had a case of the blues and was making calls to Sara that went unanswered. Danny was drinking more than ever, sitting around the galley table with Boyd, or playing pool at the Rainbird Bar. Nora was right about Danny being a chameleon, changing color to fit his surroundings. With Toby and Nick, Danny was quick and helpful and a fountain of stories, but when he was with Boyd, the talk was all guns and cars, tits and ass.

After the next opener Buddy decided to call it a season. They headed back to Petersburg where they ran the seine over the block one last time, stopping to pick it clean of every bit of slime and kelp. They stored the seine in a locker on the second floor of a huge gear shed, dragging stretch after stretch of web, lead line, and cork line across the floor, then dousing the pile with detergent to keep the rats away.

Late afternoon they headed south with the *Guinevere* in tow. Nick left Petersburg as he had arrived three months before, sitting on his dead troller staring at the stern of a seiner. They reached Wrangell in the dark of night and moored the *Guinevere* alongside the *Arlice*, an old seiner with a bank foreclosure notice taped to its galley door.

In slashing wind and driving rain, Nick stopped at Milly's Café the next afternoon, but Nora was not there. On his way to the post office, he lingered in front of Angerman's store and listened to the rain drum on the overhead awning as he watched a big cruise ship come alongside the city dock. The tug crew was having a hard time with the wind. October now, this had to be the last cruise ship of the year, a laggard that should have departed for the Caribbean with the other birds of passage.

Despite the weather, the town had sent out a welcoming committee that included a brass band whose members looked as though they had been dragged from school by the scruffs of their necks. The forlorn tuba played counterpoint to the hooting of the tug. Alongside the band, a line of cancan dancers dressed in black satin and scarlet sashes did high kicks. They could have been the musicians' mothers. The slab sides of the big ship towered above; only a few passengers had braved the storm to stand along the rail mummified in rain slickers.

When the gangplank was in place, the passengers began to trickle ashore and the band retreated, heads bowed against the rain. The dancers followed, feathers drooping like a band of guinea fowl caught in a downpour. Nonetheless the ladies were laughing. The fourth in line was Nora.

"Oops, this is embarrassing," she said when she caught Nick's eye. "I feel like a little girl caught raiding her mother's closet."

"So this is your new calling," Nick said. The other ladies gave him a quick, summarizing glance and moved on.

"Not always. One of the Shady Ladies called in sick and I got drafted. Problem with coming back to your hometown—everybody thinks they own a piece of you." She shook her head, water flying.

"You want my coat?" Nick started to remove his green wool halibut jacket, which also glistened with rain.

"I'm soaked already. I gotta get into something dry. Come have a cup of tea."

Together they walked along the waterfront road; Nora took Nick's arm to avoid the potholes. "High heels and bad roads," she said.

"Sounds like a country and western song."

"Everything does after two weeks in Milly's Café."

A man passed them with scarcely a glance. Maybe it was a common sight in Wrangell, Nick thought—a man in rubber boots and wool jacket escorting a sopping wet lady in a short black dress and feathered headband. Nick remembered the bar in Whitehorse, the Native man with the lady in the formal gown. Somehow he had become what he had once found bizarre. Was that the arc of time Sara had talked about on the barge, what seemed like a long time ago?

Nora had a downstairs apartment in a big frame house that overlooked the water. She led the way up the narrow sidewalk that traversed the garden at the back of the house. Nick studied the way her calf muscles tensed as she climbed in the high heels.

Nora was shaking with cold. Once inside she said, "You deal with the tea, I've got to get warm."

Nick rummaged in the kitchen. As he made the tea he listened to the shower run. He took a mug and sat in an easy chair by the front window. The apartment was shabbier than the one in Petersburg, but somehow it felt as though Nora was living there instead of just camping out.

Nora came from the bedroom barefoot in a heavy bathrobe, toweling her hair vigorously. She looked at Nick—his sunburn had faded a bit and he looked less tired. She was surprised how much her heart had jumped when she saw him on Front Street. She hoped she had not looked too ridiculous in the cancan outfit.

"So how's your daughter?" Nick asked.

"Coping."

"No big changes?"

"She's kind of in a holding pattern now. The changes will come later. And they won't all be good." Duane had asked Trish if he could move back in. Nora had advised her to get off that merry-go-round before it went too fast.

"Still Miss Perpetual Sunshine, aren't you?" Nick laughed.

Nora shrugged. "Where's Toby?"

"On the boat, weighing his options."

"Which are?"

"Well, Danny gave him a list of skippers out west to contact. Crab boats. But this morning he got a letter from Sara Quan. She wants Toby to share an apartment with her next semester."

"Oh, brother. I don't know which would be more dangerous. Crabbing out of Dutch or living with Miss Quan."

Nick looked through the misted window at the rain hammering the ocean. Sea and sky at war with one another. Living with Sara would be difficult, but there might be compensations, indeed there might.

"I know what you're thinking," Nora said.

"Hey, I was only wondering, what's the worst when you really want something—to miss it or to get it?"

"Probably the worst is not to try at all."

Nick watched a pickup loaded with slab wood drive slowly by, its wheels throwing spray from the potholes. "I don't know why that makes me think of Danny Sullivan," he said.

"Danny, the born loser. He'll end up in prison one way or another."

"He's a good friend, though."

"So long as you watch your back. You still planning to go shrimping this winter?"

"Me and Buddy and Danny."

"The three musketeers."

"Over the hill gang, more like. What's the shelf life on swashbuckling?"

"Depends on the package." Nora looked at Nick. Maybe he represented more squandered talent than either Buddy or Danny, but more and more she thought that a deep kindness was his most enduring feature. Which made up for a lot of shortcomings.

"You gonna live on the boat this winter?" she asked.

"The *Lily* or the *Guinevere*, yeah."

"It's tough living in the harbor in winter. Cold, and you never really dry out."

"Oh, well . . ." Nick's voice trailed away and there was another awkward silence. Nora stood up and pulled her bathrobe tightly around her. She walked over to Nick's chair and sat down in his lap. She ran her fingers through his thick, curly hair.

"Move in with me, Nick," she said.

Toby walked home along empty streets. He had sat alone at the Stikine Inn bar till closing time, avoiding the damp of the harbor, the loneliness of the boat. Streetlights glinted in the puddles along Front Street. Someone stumbled out of the Brig bar, took a few unsteady

steps, and fell. Toby rushed to help and found that it was Buddy Stepovich, hatless, his hair awry.

"My car keys," Buddy mumbled, crawling on his hands and knees.
"Can't find my car keys."

"I don't think you drove, skipper." Toby helped him to his feet. "You
want to go to the boat?"

"Oh, yeah, the boat. The beautiful *Lily.* 'S not my boat, 's Milo's boat."

Toby put an arm under Buddy's shoulders and began to steer him
toward the harbor. He could feel Buddy's ribs through his thin jacket,
slatted like venetian blinds.

CHAPTER 22

The mud flats N of Wrangell Island, at the mouth
of the Stikine River from Kadin Island to Gerard
Point are very dynamic and have a tendency to
migrate seaward. Mariners are advised to use
extreme caution when navigating in these areas
due to the constantly changing nature of the bottom.
—US Coast Pilot

"The fuckin' ducks, man."

"Ducks?"

"They're everywhere. The flats are fuckin' crawling with 'em. We could fill the freezer in an hour."

"I don't know."

Danny and Nick were rigging shrimp pots. Buddy had gone uptown to call the boat broker, and Toby had headed for the coffee shop. Danny was trying to promote a hunting trip to the Stikine Flats, selling it hard.

"C'mon," he said cajolingly.

"I never hunted much," Nick said. "Growing up in Detroit, people mostly shot each other."

"Ducks aren't any different. I've got a skiff we can use. And a tent."

"Sounds cold."

"C'mon, it'll be a fuckin' lark."

"So you decided to go out west," Nora said to Toby.

"I got a ticket to Dutch next week."

"I hope it's the right call." Nora refilled his coffee cup.

"I can still make it back for second semester. I've got till January. Anyway, there's nobody to talk to on the *Lily* now that Nick's otherwise engaged." Toby grinned at Nora. Nick had been reluctant to admit where he was going when he moved his gear up to Nora's apartment. Toby had teased Nick till he blushed, but Nora would not rise to the bait.

"With Nick, the only thing engaged is his mouth," she said.

"You gonna fix Danny up with one of your friends?"

Nora looked down the counter. Two of her old high school buddies sat talking with Milly about the previous day's soap operas, a Greek chorus sitting in judgment on imaginary beings. "You think I'd betray my own gender?" Nora said.

"Hey, c'mon. Danny's a good guy."

"If you say so."

Toby spun his coffee cup and thought of Sara. When she had suggested they share an apartment, she had stipulated "just as friends." How was that going to work?

"Old fishermen are such loners," he said. "Has Danny ever had a girlfriend you know of?"

"He said the cook on the *Hero* used to be his girl."

"Melody? The one that went overboard? But . . ." Toby hesitated.

"What?"

"I don't know. Billy, or maybe it was Aaron . . . no, Billy, said she had a big fight with Sven the night she went over. The way he said it, it sounded like a lover's quarrel."

"Probably was. If she was choosy about who she slept with she wouldn't have been on that boat."

Toby looked down at his coffee, and Nora suddenly remembered Sara on the boat. Her big mouth, always getting her in trouble, always. She went down to freshen the coffee of her two friends. They said something to her, but she was not listening. She was certain she had never heard mention of a last night quarrel for Melody. Could that be a piece in the jigsaw puzzle? Or was it a puzzle at all? Somehow she could not let go of the image of Melody's losing hope in the cold ocean as the boat moved on. But that may have been her own fear of dying alone.

Nick and Danny walked through the door, bringing cold air and laughter. "Hey, we're going hunting," Nick said as they sat down.

"Moose?" Nora asked, pouring more coffee.

"Ducks," Danny said, "on the flats."

"Only thing I ever hunted was pheasants," Nick said. "With some fraternity brothers in Kalamazoo."

"Kalamazoo?" Danny questioned the existence of such a place.

"A, B, C, D, E, F, G, H, I got a gal in Kalamazoo-zoo-zoo," Nick sang, beating time with his spoon against his cup. The ladies at the end of the counter stopped talking and looked his way. Nora wanted to announce that she did not actually know these guys, but then Buddy came through the door and sat down.

"Any word from the broker?" Nick asked him.

"Sven Oslund made an offer on the *Lily*," Buddy said in a low voice. They all fell silent.

"What does he want her for?" Toby asked.

"I guess he's got a nephew in Sitka he wants to help get started."

"Sven Oslund? Help somebody?" Nora said. "Well, ex-*cuse* me."

"I know the kid," Danny said. "I hate to say it, but he's a comer. He might make Sven some money."

They all fell silent again.

"You going hunting with the boys?" Nora asked Buddy.

"Hunting?"

"Yeah, ducks. Over on Farm Island," Danny said. "Come on. I can borrow another skiff, and you and Toby can take it."

Buddy looked into his coffee cup. "Let's take the *Lily*," he said.

"The *Lily*? On the flats? Are you crazy?"

"The old man used to do it."

"I'm going, too," Nora said impulsively.

"Wind doesn't help. It confuses the picture." Buddy gripped the wheel, a cigarette clenched between his teeth.

"I can't tell a bleedin' thing," Nick said. He was keeping Buddy company on the flying bridge. Ahead was the lumpy outline of Farm Island, but off to starboard there were visible sand bars.

Nick looked back at the mud churning in their wake. They were towing Danny's river skiff, and on the *Lily's* back deck was a borrowed green fiberglass canoe. The deck looked large and empty without the seine or the seine skiff.

"Me and the old man used to come out here a lot when I was a kid," Buddy said. "Back then everybody had a locker at the cold storage full of ducks, and we'd hunt moose up the Stikine and deer over on Etolin. Wrangell was real isolated, you had to shift for yourself."

"How about vegetables? And milk?"

"Everybody had a garden. And there were a few farms. One on this island."

"Hence the name."

"Yeah. But there was one in Wrangell too. You've seen that street named Cow Alley? They used to take the cows down to the waterfront, to graze on salt grass. But that's all gone now."

Buddy followed a channel that the river had scoured from King Slough across the Koknuk Flats. With one hand on the wheel and one on the throttle, he eased the *Lily* between Dry Island and Little Dry Island till he found deeper water. He throttled back till the *Lily* seemed motionless relative to the land, facing into the current. Danny Sullivan went forward and dropped the hook.

"Safe haven," Buddy said.

"Pasta Puttanesca," Nora said to Toby as she added anchovies and chilies to the sauce.

"What's that mean?"

"Whore's spaghetti."

"Already it's my favorite," Toby said.

Danny looked in the galley door for a moment, then headed to the back deck to light another cigarette. Danny had delayed their departure till they almost missed the tide. He had been on the phone to Petersburg and came back morose and angry. For a week he had been trying to wring his crew share out of Sven. Or so he said.

After dinner Buddy polished his shotgun with Hoppe's oil. The gun was a double-barrel Browning 12 gauge with an engraved receiver and a cloudy bit of burl on the walnut stock. He broke it open and stared down the barrels.

"Jesus, that's a beautiful gun," Danny said. "Must be Milo's."

"Yeah," Buddy said. "I haven't owned a gun in years. Mom sneaked it out of the closet for me."

"Must have cost a fuckin' ton."

"The old man, he always liked fancy gear. Boats, guns, women, cars, he was always strutting his stuff."

"Milo, I used to hear more stories about him out on the grounds. Great fuckin' fisherman," Danny said.

"He grew up with the industry. Started out beach seining in front of Ballard Locks when he was a kid. With a steam winch. Then he worked all the way up to the age of GPS and color sonar."

"Bet he hated that modern shit."

"Not really," Buddy shook his head. "He had to have the best gear, the best tools. He was always ready to spend money on gear."

"He was tough on his crew, though," Danny said. "Use 'em up and throw 'em away. No deposit, no return. No respect, either. I hated working for him."

"That's the old man all right. Hard on people." Buddy snapped the Browning shut.

Early next morning they went ashore—Danny, Buddy, and Toby in the skiff, Nick and Nora in the green canoe. They beached the boats by the saltwater creek that divided Farm Island and Little Dry Island and then split up, planning to walk the beach and jump shoot the ponds.

The sun cleared the Coast Range and cast long shadows on the frozen grass. Nick and Nora came to a pothole and a dozen mallards sprang into the air with a flurry of wings. Nora swung on them, shot, pumped, and shot again. A single bird fell. Nick did not fire.

"This is a nice gun," Nora said, replacing the two spent shells. She was shooting a 16 gauge Ithaca that belonged to Buddy's mother. "Beautiful balance. Why didn't you shoot?"

"I don't know."

Walking again they bumped shoulders. "Sorry," Nick said. They were still a little tentative around each other, physically. The mutual history of failed relationships made them both wary.

They came upon another pothole, its surface flecked with mallards and goldeneyes. When the birds flew, Nora shot three times but missed. Then a single green-winged teal was up and away much more quickly than the mallards. Nick swung and fired, and it folded in midair, tumbling.

"Jeez," Nora said in admiration. Maybe wing shooting was like hitting a baseball, same hand-eye coordination. How could Nick do difficult things so effortlessly and still be such a screw-up?

Nick spoke not a word but stroked the duck's glossy neck, then spread one wing as if considering the intricacy of flight. When the bird tumbled from the sky, he had felt a jolt in his own stomach.

Nora shot one more mallard, but after that they just walked. A bit of wind skirled around the edges of the day, driving dust devils across the exposed sandbars. They heard the distant drone of an outboard.

"More hunters?" Nick said.

"It's moose season. Hope they're okay. I think the weather's going to get dirty, and the flats are an awful place for a small boat." She shivered and stuck her hands in her pockets. "One of Buck's best friends died out here, moose hunting. He lost the channel and went aground, and the waves basically beat him to death. The year after that three high school boys drowned. They found one body tied to their skiff; the other two were just gone."

"At least we've got the *Lily*."

"I'm not sure she'd be much better. I don't know what Buddy was thinking, bringing her out here. Almost a death wish."

"Could be his last trip with her."

"That asshole Milo, it's not like he needs the money. He should just give the boat to Buddy. Maybe he'll die before the sale goes through. He's already had one stroke."

"If Milo's anything like I hear, he'll hang on till Buddy dies first."

Nora puzzled over that idea. High overhead she saw a flock of sandhill cranes, like pencil marks against the cirrus clouds. She could hear their rusty gate voices. End of the season, end of something more.

"Cranes mate for life, don't they?" she said in a low voice.

"You asking me?"

"Fourteen," Danny said. "How'd you do?"

"Three."

"Three? What were you lovebirds up to?" Danny held a plucked duck over the flames of a small beach fire, singeing the pinfeathers. Toby was plucking ducks by the water's edge; Buddy was cleaning one of the singed ducks. In the firelight their faces glowed like goblins.

"How many you got ready?" Nora asked. "I could go out to the boat and start cooking."

A skiff appeared, coming down channel, its wake silvery in the dark. It turned and beached next to their skiff and canoe. A man ran an anchor ashore and stomped it in the mud. The tillerman walked forward into the firelight: Sven Oslund, wearing camouflage gear and hip boots with their tops turned down around his knees.

"Fuckin' cold." Sven hunkered down and held his hands over the fire. Aaron was with him, wearing a stocking cap and dark raingear. He hung back as though more comfortable in the shadows.

"Where'd you two spring from?" Danny asked.

"Moose hunting." Sven jerked a thumb upriver. He looked at Buddy. "We seen the *Lily* on the flats. Couldn't believe it. You've got balls like a brass monkey."

"We used to do it all the time," Buddy said.

"Wrangell guys." Sven shook his head as though considering a particularly disreputable tribe. "My nephew tries something like that with the *Lily*, I'll kick his ass."

He scratched his backside. "The broker tells me you made a counteroffer."

Buddy nodded without speaking.

"Ain't gonna work," Sven said. "I figure Milo'd rather anybody but you had her."

Buddy dropped the duck he was cleaning and looked at Sven, his hands bloody in the firelight.

"Hey, no offense. Everybody knows it couldn't've been easy, having a ballbreaker like Milo for your old man." Sven nudged a stick farther into the fire. "Look, I've been meaning to apologize for corking you that day at Noyes Island. It was a bad day."

"Forget it," Buddy said. "That stuff happens all the time. Nobody remembers it."

"I got my comeuppance anyway," Sven laughed. "Looked like a fool. Then to top it off, your crewman goes and throws me in the harbor." He looked at Toby and laughed again as if to show there were no hard feelings. He reached into his back pocket and pulled out a pint of whiskey. "Peace offering?" he said.

"No, thanks," Buddy said.

"C'mon. This is good stuff." Sven reached out and poured a slug in Buddy's coffee mug. "It won't even give you a headache."

"I hate to break this up," Nora said suddenly, "but I've really got to get out to the boat and start cooking." She had had about all she could stomach of Sven Oslund.

"Wanna stay and eat with us?" Buddy asked Sven.

"Duck dinner?" Sven looked to where Aaron sat just at the edge of the light, cleaning his fingernails with a pocketknife. "Whaddaya say, Aaron?"

"Suits me," Aaron closed the knife.

Ice on the metal thwarts of the green canoe. Seven plucked ducks in the bottom. Nora wielded the bow paddle with vehemence.

"That bastard," she said as they entered the warmth of the galley. "Trying to get Buddy drunk."

"Buddy could always say no, nobody's forcing him," Nick said mildly.

"Jee-*sus*!" Nora was fed up with men and their macho games. And the nice ones like Nick and Toby just stood by and did nothing. She chopped an apple, wielding the knife so fiercely that a slice flew half way across the galley.

"What are the apples for?" Nick asked.

"They absorb some of the grease when the ducks roast." Nora took a head of garlic and began to cut the cloves into thin slivers. Nick opened a bottle of wine and brought her a glass. She put the ducks in a roasting pan and slammed the oven door on them, then took her glass of wine to the back deck.

A few stars were visible through the torn canopy of clouds. On-shore she could see dark figures moving against the firelight. The tide was slack but the river's flow still rippled the waters of the slough. The *Lily* moved uneasily to the touch of the current

Five men in hunting clothes crowded around the galley table. Toby sat on a stool, his long legs propped against a bulkhead. Sven ran his hand across the varnished woodwork in proprietary fashion.

"Beautiful fuckin' boat," he said. "They don't make 'em like this anymore."

"The old man's pride and joy," Buddy said, his voice a little slurred. He gestured with one hand and knocked over his mug. Whiskey sloshed on the tabletop.

"Plenty more where that came from," Sven said. He cracked the seal on another bottle, a fifth of Jameson, and filled Buddy's cup.

Without a word Nora placed the ducks on the table along with a pot of rice. The men ate avidly, except for Buddy who stared at his plate as though pondering what he should do with it. Nora leaned against the kitchen counter, picking at a duck breast, still furious.

"Ouch." Sven reached into his mouth, pried out a bit of shot and looked at it. "Number fours," he said. "Damn, that duck was good, Nora. Sara Quan, she would've spread ginger or some shit all over it." He looked at Toby. "You heard from Sara?"

"One letter."

"I sent her a settlement check, but she never wrote back."

Nora rolled her eyes. What was he expecting, a thank-you note for the black eye?

"I guess you had a tough year for crew," she said sweetly.

"Deckhands." Sven shook his head. "Always a headache."

"Melody drowned, Billy choked to death, Sara beaten up." Nora ticked off her fingers. "That's a headache?"

"Nobody said it was easy out there," Sven said, an answer that further infuriated Nora.

"I heard you and Melody had a big fight the night she went over. Think the Coast Guard might be interested in that?"

"Melody?" Sven looked genuinely puzzled. "The last I saw her was her last crappy supper. Didn't know she was gone till Danny told me."

Nora stopped short, trying to figure how this fit the picture, if it was true. "Two weeks till the Coast Guard hearing, isn't it?" she said.

"Naah, I got it postponed till after the halibut opener."

"I always wanted to go to one. It could get interesting."

Sven shrugged, but Aaron looked at Nora. He, too, took a piece of shot from his mouth and dropped it on his plate—a sharp ring of metal on china.

CHAPTER 23

*Dry Island and Farm Island are on the
E side of Dry Strait NNE of Blaquiere Point.
Boats should not attempt passage between
these islands. A poor channel can be followed
at high tide between Farm Island and Sergief
Island to the S.*

—*US Coast Pilot*

An outboard motor roared into life beside the *Lily,* the noise quickly fading northbound. Nora sat up in her bunk and grabbed her clothes. She had gone to bed before the others and now expected to find the galley looking like the wreckage of harmony and order. However, Nick had gotten up before her, and the table was clean and wiped, and he was just finishing the dishes. Nora felt a surge of gratitude, mixed with irritation at the loss of an opportunity to feel superior.

"Morning," Nick said.

"I overslept. When did those bozos leave?"

"Real late."

"How's Buddy?"

"Passed out in his cabin. When I looked in I thought he was dead. I put a blanket over him and checked his pulse. It was real fluttery."

"Bastards," Nora said vehemently. "Who took the skiff?"

"Danny. He didn't say where he was going. Didn't say a word, he looked pretty bad himself."

Toby stumbled up from the fo'c'sle. Without a word he filled a cup with water, drank it, filled it again, drank it, filled it again, turned, and said, "Morning." A gust of wind caused the boat to swing on its anchor.

"This better blow itself out by tomorrow or we're gonna be stranded," Nora said. "I doubt even Buddy'd be able to find the channel in this."

An hour later Toby and Nick launched the canoe on the lee side of the *Lily*. Nora stood by, wearing a parka and stocking cap, the Ithaca cradled in her forearms.

"No guns?" she asked the boys.

"I'm not in a killing mood," Nick said.

"Is everybody from Michigan a closet Buddhist?"

Neither answered, both obviously suffering from hangovers. Nora felt a little smug about her clear head and focused eyes. On the short paddle to the beach, the canoe shipped a little water in the stiff chop. Toby chose to walk the beach alone while Nick and Nora cut into the woods.

"What are we looking for?" Nick asked.

"Blue grouse. Hooters."

"Hooters?"

"In the spring they make this soft hooting call. Like blowing across a beer bottle."

"They anything like ruffed grouse?"

"Bigger. Just as dumb, just as tasty."

They quartered uphill. The wind soughed in the tall trees. "I wonder where those other guys got to," Nick said. "Sven and Aaron, I mean. And Danny."

"Wherever it is, I don't want to go there."

"You were pulling Sven's chain pretty hard, last night."

"I'm gonna pull it even harder."

"You might want to use a little caution, dealing with those two."

"Caution? Nick, that's for school crossings."

A grouse started up beneath their feet and then glided on stiff wings through the spruce. A difficult shot but Nora swung and pulled the trigger and the bird fell. It was newly fledged and so small she was able to stuff it in the pocket of her parka. She felt a sudden twinge of regret.

Buddy woke in his bunk. Clad only in boxer shorts, he walked unsteadily to the galley. A pot of coffee sat on the back of the stove and he poured himself a cup, but the bitter, burnt taste made him bend over the sink and retch. He wiped his mouth; blood stained the back of his hand.

He opened a cupboard, looking for the bottle of Pepto-Bismol but instead found the Jameson bottle, still holding three inches of whiskey. He unscrewed the cap and sniffed.

"Where the fuck's my share?" Danny was not asking about fish money.

"You walked away. You get nothing," Sven held his shotgun cradled in his arms.

"It was my idea, my connection. I'm the one who set it up with the Samoans." Danny looked to Aaron who sat on a drift log, holding his own gun. "Aaron, you tell him. That's the way the deal goes down."

"Honor among thieves?" Aaron spat out his toothpick. "Did you tell that woman what we were doing?"

"Nora? Hell no," Danny said uneasily. "She's got a hard-on about Melody, you know that."

"Fuck," Aaron said and slowly stood up. "You already ratted us out, didn't you?"

Sven heard movement in the brush. He turned and saw someone break onto the beach about twenty-five yards away—that lanky kid, Toby. Sven made a shushing motion at Aaron and Danny, but they were locked in a stare-down.

"Danny, Danny," Aaron shook his head. "You are such a little rat. I should've remembered from Walla Walla." He poked Danny in the chest with his shotgun. "You know there ain't nothin' gonna make me go back inside."

"Fuck you." Danny knocked the barrel away, but Aaron reversed the gun and slammed the butt into Danny's chest, knocking him backward onto the sand.

Danny rolled over and struggled to his knees, coughing raggedly. Looking up at Aaron's mean smile, he had a sudden insight that this might have been the very last thing Melody had ever seen. "Jesus," he said with a strangled voice. "It was you Billy heard arguing with Melody, wasn't it? You fuckin' dirt bag—"

"Be sure to say hello for us," Aaron racked the pump and leveled the gun.

"What the hell—" Sven started to say just as Toby came full tilt across the beach and tackled Aaron, rolling him in the sand. Toby wrenched the shotgun free and heaved it toward the water's edge.

Aaron crawled back, pulled a knife, and snapped it open. He got to his feet and grinned at Toby. "C'mon, college boy, I bet your pussy's softer than your girlfriend's." He made a little carving motion with the knife.

Toby ignored the taunt but squared off, completely intent, his hands held open at chest height. Aaron feinted with the knife, feinted again. Toby took a step backward as if retreating but suddenly stooped and grabbed a handful of sand and threw it at Aaron's face. Aaron brought an arm up to shield his eyes, and Toby lunged and hit him hard, a right cross to the body, but Aaron slashed down with the knife, just nicking Toby's forearm and drawing blood.

Toby stepped back and brought his hands up again. He circled to his left, still not saying a word and not even glancing at the blood welling from his forearm.

"Goddamn it, Aaron, knock this shit off," Sven said but made no move to get between them. Aaron feinted with the knife again, but then a rock flew out of the woods and hit him square in the side of the head, driving him to one knee.

"Motherfucker!" Aaron yelled. He put his hand up to his head and the fingers came away bloody.

Danny was gone, vanished. Sven looked toward the woods and saw Nick and Nora. Nick's arm was cocked again but his second rock missed as Aaron scrabbled down the beach toward his gun.

"Toby!" Nora screamed as Aaron reached the gun. Toby hesitated but then turned and sprinted toward the woods. A third rock hit Aaron in the back, but he swiveled and fired from the hip as Toby disappeared into the trees. Aaron turned toward Nick and Nora and fired again, but they were also gone.

Sven looked at the bright red shotgun shells on the shingled beach. He had the sensation that he was falling down the surface of a steep wave that was about to break. There was a faint odor of gunpowder, and the shots still seemed to reverberate in the air.

Blood trickled down Aaron's cheekbone. He threw his shotgun

down in the riverboat and picked up his rifle. "You fucking asshole," he screamed at Sven. "Why didn't you shoot?"

When the second shot tore through the spruce branches, Nick was already running, following Nora as she forced her way through the devil's club and began to climb the steep hillside. When they reached the top of the ridge, Nora slumped down behind a tree, taking deep, ragged breaths. Her clothes were covered with pine duff, and her face was gray with effort, two white spots on her cheekbones. "I gotta rest a second," she said, pressing one hand to her side.

Nick's breathing slowed, and once again he could hear the creak of trees moving, the sough of wind in the branches overhead. A movement on his left startled him, but then he saw it was Toby, slipping through the trees to join them.

"You all right?" Nick asked him.

"I think so." Toby's eyes were wide, his face pale, a line of blood marking his wrist.

"Where's Danny?"

"Dunno. What's this all about?"

"No idea. But we better not stick around to ask."

A rifle cracked and a bullet whined overhead. Nora shot back, then all three were running pell-mell down the back side of the ridge. They broke out onto the beach only a few yards from their canoe. Offshore the *Lily* pointed into the rising wind, her anchor chain taut.

Nick and Toby grabbed the canoe by the gunwales and ran it into the water. No one spoke, but they all seemed to share the idea of getting to the *Lily* as quickly as possible. Nora sat in the middle. The green wall of trees was already too far away for her shotgun but an easy rifle shot. What in God's name was going on?

They rounded the stern of the *Lily* and came along her port side, sheltered from the beach. Toby sprang aboard with the painter, nearly swamping the canoe, and Nick and Nora followed.

They found Buddy sprawled facedown on the galley table. The empty whiskey bottle lay on its side and beside it stood a half-empty bottle of wine. "Oh, Jesus," Nora said. She grabbed Buddy by the shirtfront and slapped him hard, his head lolling. Toby pushed by her and went down to the engine room, and soon they heard the rumble of the main engine starting. Toby came back up the companionway and closed the engine room door. The noise lessened and life seemed almost normal.

"Why were we running?" Nick said. "Maybe there's some explanation."

Toby frowned. "If you'd seen the look in Aaron's eyes, you wouldn't be asking."

"But, still."

"Nick, they were shooting at us," Nora said exasperatedly. "And that was a rifle the second time. I don't know what this is all about, but if we just sit here we're fucked."

"What about Danny?" Nick looked toward the shore.

"We don't even know what side he's on," said Nora.

"We gotta move. Now." Toby took charge. "I'll get the anchor. Nick, you take the wheel."

Toby headed forward along the port side, keeping the wheelhouse between him and the shore. Nick started toward the flying bridge, but Nora grabbed his sleeve.

"Don't go up there, Nick."

"I can't see from down here."

"Nick—" Nora said and plucked at his sleeve again. "Look, I'll get Buddy up, just give me a minute."

Nick shook his head and turned and went forward to the lower steering station. Through the rain-streaked windows he saw the anchor slam home against the cathead, silty mud on its flukes. The *Lily* was drifting backward now, starting to turn sideways to the wind. In the poor light, all he could see was a troubled line of waves. He put the boat in the gear and cautiously opened the throttle.

Nora partly filled the deck bucket and threw the seawater in Buddy's face. He sat up spluttering, "Whaaat—" and at that moment the galley window shattered, glass falling in the sink as they heard a distant bang. Nora instinctively ducked away. A second bullet slammed into the wheelhouse.

Then the *Lily*'s keel touched bottom, a light touch followed by a harder bump. Nick opened the throttle wide and the *Lily* forced her way free, the stern slewing slightly as she sought deeper water. For a few second there was clear sailing, and Nora let out a sigh of relief, but then the *Lily* struck hard, climbing a mud bank and tilting sharply to port. The wine bottle fell off the table and broke; green glass and red wine mixed with window glass and seawater.

Nick killed the engine. Silence now, except for the thud of waves against the hull. Nora leaned against a slanting bulkhead, stuck her hands in the pockets of her parka, and almost jumped at the unexpected touch of feathers. She pulled the dead grouse from her pocket. The closed eyelids were a pale blue.

"What the fuck you think you're doing?" Sven yelled as he broke from the woods, panting heavily.

"I thought I might scare 'em into running aground. It worked." Aaron lifted his rifle and fired twice more at the *Lily* even though she was now beyond effective range.

"Are you out of your mind?" Sven bent over to ease the stitch in his side. His face was red as a crab shell after scrambling across the ridge in hip boots and heavy wool clothing.

"How long you think they'll be there?" Aaron asked.

"Maybe forever." Sven straightened and looked toward the *Lily*. A wave broke against her bow and she seemed to slew a bit on the mud. "She could pound to pieces if this wind keeps up."

"Good."

"Did Danny make it on board?"

"Danny?" Aaron looked startled. "I forgot about that little prick. He coulda doubled back and taken the skiffs." Aaron turned and began to race back up the hillside. Sven watched him go, shaking his head. Goddamn crewmen always caused trouble, always. At the end of the season you should put them all in a bag and toss them overboard, like stray cats. But this mess was way out of the ordinary. He turned and looked at the *Lily*, not a sign of life onboard. If only he could get out there and explain things. Not that he owed anybody an apology. Melody, this had all started with Melody. What had Danny meant about Aaron being the last one she saw? And what was the big deal anyway? Some scrawny junkie takes a brodie off his boat and it turns into this major shitstorm? Sven shook his head and turned and followed Aaron.

Nora looked out the galley door. The beach was empty. A cloud of seagulls hovered above the channel. Their wings beat steadily, but they remained stationary, pointing into the still rising wind. Suddenly onshore someone waved a jacket to signal the *Lily*.

"It's Danny," Toby said, looking through binoculars. "We'd better go get him."

"Over my dead body. You've got no idea what kind of game he's playing."

"Nora, it's Danny," Nick said, as if that explained something. He and Toby grabbed the paddles and climbed into the canoe

"Nick! Goddammit, Nick!" Nora shouted, but they pushed off, quartering into the ugly seas. "Toby!" she yelled this time, but neither looked back. If they didn't drown, they'd probably get shot. What if this was a Trojan horse gimmick? Nora remembered how hard Danny had sold the hunting trip. Had he already arranged to meet Sven out here? In frustration, Nora slammed her head back against the doorjamb so hard that it stung. Goddamn all men. Goddamn every single worthless one of them.

Buddy found a bit of plywood that he taped over the broken window. Daylight still bled through the listing portside window, but it was fading fast. With the boat canted over, they could not run the generator, and Nora lit a candle and placed it on the table as they sat waiting. As the candle flickered, shadows crossed Buddy's face. Each time a wave struck the bow, he shuddered along with the *Lily*.

After what seemed an interminable wait, Nora heard the canoe bump against the hull. A moment later Danny Sullivan stood in the door.

"Howdy, shipmates," he said.

CHAPTER 24

The channels of the S arm of the Stikine River
are followed by experienced boatmen by the
appearance of the water. No permanent
directions can be given since the channel across
the mud flats at the mouth of the river changes
with every freshet.

—US Coast Pilot

"Took your time, didn't you?" Aaron said as Sven walked down the beach. Aaron sat on the bow of their riverboat. Danny's skiff lay alongside, tethered now to the riverboat's stern. Sven put his gun in its case and threw it angrily in the bottom of the boat.

"What the fuck difference does it make?" Sven was irked that Aaron no longer remembered who was the boss. "I can find my way back to Petersburg in the dark if I have to. Wind or no fuckin' wind."

"Petersburg? Who said anything about Petersburg?"

"Where the fuck else we gonna go?"

"We got a job to finish. No loose ends. Comprende?"

Sven looked at him but said nothing.

"What's the matter, pussy? Cold feet?"

"Look, I'm the captain—"

"The captain? Of fuckin' what?" Aaron spat angrily in the water. "Shit, it's a piece of cake. If their boat doesn't pound to pieces, we burn it. Swamp their skiff, and it'll look like they went aground, then drowned trying to get away. Piece of fuckin' cake."

"I signed on to some idiot drug deal, not this other bullshit." Sven picked up the bow and shoved the skiff into the water, forcing Aaron to jump to his feet. "Easy money, you said. You and Danny Sullivan, I hope you both fuckin' rot in prison."

"You think you're gonna get off free? You wanna stay out of the slam? We gotta end this now."

"Fuck you." Sven climbed into the boat and started the engine. "I'm headed home. You can spend the night on the beach if you want to. It's all the same to me."

Aaron hesitated, then hopped in the bow. Sven opened the throttle and turned the boat in a long curve, Danny's skiff trailing on its painter. Once out of the cove the wind and seas increased. Sven ducked his head against the spray. Despite his bravado, he knew it would be a tough trip back to Petersburg.

Aaron huddled in the bow, his stocking cap pulled low. Sven watched him take a pint of whisky from his vest pocket, pull the cork with his teeth, and take a swig. Jesus, what a psycho, Sven thought. How had he let himself get talked into this? He had always been a winner, always. Sven looked down at the dented green metal of his riverboat, at the red gas can, the blue cooler containing their food. All the familiar tackle of a hunting trip, how had it come to be part of a nightmare?

The engine stuttered and almost died. Sven shut it off and nudged the gas tank—empty. In a towering rage he yanked the fuel line free and grabbed another five-gallon tank. He knelt in the bilge and squeezed the priming bulb. The wife, Sven thought, this was all her fault, the bitch. If she had stayed home like she was supposed to, none of this would have happened.

Sven pulled the cord and the big Mercury came back to life. They had drifted backward, and the skiff's painter was now fouled on the lower unit. Sven bent over the stern to free the line. As he did so he heard Aaron rack the slide of his shotgun, and Sven realized that he had made a very big mistake. He threw himself sideways as Aaron pulled the trigger. Sven grabbed the tiller for balance and inadvertently twisted the throttle open. The skiff turned sharply at full throttle, dipping one rail, and Sven went backward over the transom.

Aaron scrambled back to the stern as the skiff returned to an even keel. He could see Sven, struggling to swim toward Danny's skiff, burdened by his heavy clothing. Aaron opened the throttle again, and the painter came taut and Danny's skiff yawed and twitched away from Sven's reach. Aaron towed it in a long, slow curve, watching Sven's head barely above the water, shouting something that Aaron could not make out. Then only Sven's arm was above the water, fingers outstretched, grasping. And then nothing broke the shifting plane of the surface.

"The *Green Hornet*," Danny said.

"The *Green Hornet*?" Nick wrinkled his brow.

"Yeah."

"What kind of name is that for a boat?"

"Trollers, they're not what you'd call normal," Danny said. "Anyway, the guy that owns her shoots my buddy Rob, right there in Wrangell harbor, and then takes off in the boat. I mean, think about it. An old wooden boat with a dipshit name doing six knots, max. How's he gonna get away?"

"Why did he shoot the guy?" asked Toby.

"Saturday night in Wrangell, who knows? But all the state cops or the Coast Guard had to do was call the harbormasters in half a dozen little towns, tell 'em to watch out for a troller called *Green Hornet*. That's all they had to do, but still the guy gets clean away."

"They never caught him?"

"Oh, they found him five, six years later, working on the North Slope. But the moral is, don't count on any help to get us out of this."

Buddy shone his flashlight around the engine room. The *Lily* lay almost on her side now that the tide had receded. The waves no longer touched her, but if the wind was still blowing when the tide started to flood, they would have a long night of it.

Buddy sat down on a box of waste rags and turned off his flashlight. His head still pounded as the last of the alcohol quarreled in his veins, and he was having trouble thinking. He had tried the VHF radio, looking for assistance, but somehow in the melee the antenna had broken, and all he could get was static. He could not believe that Sven Oslund was associated with the gunfire. He had known Sven since he was a boy—arrogant, cocksure, pushy. A pain in the ass for sure but not a killer.

Voices came down the companionway from the galley, Danny still telling stories. Buddy shook his head; the guy never stopped spinning his line of bullshit. It must be some strange compulsion, like a bird endlessly repeating the song that marked its territory. Still, the first thing Danny had done when he had come aboard was to nail a tarp over the steeply canted hatch covers so the hold would not flood when the tide came back. Buddy had still been too drunk to think of that simple measure. Buddy clicked on his flashlight. The faces of gauges blinked back at him, all the needles registering zero.

Aaron motored slowly around the top of Dry Island and started down the slough. At least he was finally rid of all the amateurs, no more dragging that lard ass Sven along. A lone wolf, that was what he was meant to be. He had been a fool to partner up with a rat like Danny in the first place. He could just cut and run now, but Danny was the wild card. Danny could not go to the cops without getting shit all over himself, but if he backed up that Nora dame on all this talk about Melody, Danny could cop a plea, which would leave only one man in the crosshairs. That damn Melody—you take a broad to bed one time, and she thinks she owns a piece of you. Melody had found out how wrong she was.

Sara Quan was even worse. Give her a few pills and somehow she thinks *you* owe *her*. But there could be trouble from that direction. Nobody could ever prove anything about Melody, and thank God no one was even asking about Billy Nichols. But Sara, if she came out of the woodwork with some bullshit assault story . . . His word against some rich fucking college girl? He'd be back in the slam before you could say Jack Daniels.

He wished he had Sara's sweet ass in his hands right now. He'd show her who was boss. He was going to enjoy making her boyfriend beg for mercy. And that loudmouth cook and her ballplayer boyfriend. Aaron reached up and touched the swollen temple where Nick's rock had hit him. Better to burn the *Lily* like he had told Sven. Burn it like that guy on the *Investor*, only be smart enough to leave no trace. Dump the bodies and let Danny's skiff go, then take Sven's riverboat back to Mitkof. Set it adrift, walk to town, and lay low till the night ferry. He would be in Seattle while the Coast Guard still had its thumb up its ass, doing the paperwork on two more boating accidents.

Aaron grinned in the dark. Someone had once asked about the guy's motive in killing the people on the *Investor*. Aaron thought it was kind of a dumb question. He bet the guy got his rocks off; it had to be a rush, clearing the whole boat that way. But he had better wait a few hours, till their guard was down on the *Lily*. Aaron beached the two skiffs and walked up to the shelter of the trees. He found a wind-fallen tree and pulled a few pieces of wood from the splintered stump, then broke a handful of twigs from the lower branches of a small spruce. He sprinkled a little gas from Danny's spare tank on the kindling and lit it. A brief whumph of blue flame and then a smoldering, meager fire. He found a pitch-filled knob of witch's broom that made the flames flare up, illuminating the thick boles of the spruce trees.

Aaron fetched the last two long necks from the blue cooler. He quickly drank them, then fished two more empties out of the skiff's bilge. He filled all four empty bottles with gasoline. He made wicks by tearing long strips from his shirt, coating them with grease so they would burn hot and slow, then twisting them tightly into the necks of the bottles. Molotov cocktails, the Bolshevik's gift to the working man.

Full dark now. Dead low water. Aaron launched Danny's skiff; it was much smaller than the riverboat and would be easier to drag across the flats. He crossed the channel at low throttle, heading for the maze of sandbars. Back beneath the trees he could still see the glimmer of his fire, like cat eyes in the dark.

Buddy taped a five-cell Maglite to the barrel of his shotgun and climbed to the flying bridge. He sat in the rain and wind, braced against the slant of the vessel, fully sober now. He had told the crew he would watch till daylight—he had thought about rotating watches, but there was no way to do so without including Danny and, like Nora, he was not sure about Danny's standing in all this.

He clicked on the flashlight and scanned the flats, but the rain-tattered beam was swallowed by the engulfing dark. The wind was so strong it seemed to bend the light. He played the light along the *Lily's* side, checking how she lay. The bow was high and dry, but there was still water aft of amidships. The tide had not fallen as much as he had expected, the wind and rain acting as a dam for the river. The *Lily* might come off the bar as early as half flood.

The flashlight caught a faint sheen of oil and he tracked it to the standpipe for the port fuel tank. Diesel was slowly siphoning out, iridescent on the black water. Buddy thought he heard the faint whine of an outboard, and he doused the light, but he heard no more. Must have been the wind in the rigging.

Aaron dragged the skiff across a shallow spot. In the twisting channels one moment the skiff was high and dry and the next the water was halfway up his thighs. Thirty feet away a seal's head popped above the water, barely discernible in the dark, its eyes ghostly as a drowned sailor. How could it find the channel in the dark? Aaron wanted to grab his shotgun and blow the seal to kingdom come, but he knew his approach to the *Lily* had to be silent.

Finally, he could see the *Lily's* wheelhouse. He beached the skiff about sixty yards from the larger vessel. The wind brought a faint whiff of raw diesel. Spilled diesel might make things easier; maybe he could burn the boat first.

Aaron stuffed the gasoline-filled bottles in the big pockets of his hunting jacket. He stuck a .357 handgun in his belt and after a moment's consideration picked up his rifle, leaving the shotgun behind. In his left hand he carried a small trenching shovel that he intended to use as a sort of catapult.

He picked his way slowly across the water till he reached a shelf of sand that he thought was close enough. He lined up the gasoline bottles on the sand and from his pocket took out his cigarette lighter.

Nick tilted the candle and the hot wax ran onto his fingers and instantly congealed. He remembered years ago as an altar boy doing the same thing with the tall beeswax candles while the priest droned on in Latin.

Nora, asleep, leaned against his shoulder. All four were huddled around the galley table, unwilling to go to the fo'c'sle. It was cold in the galley and the light from the candle was like a razor cut on the face of the dark.

"Aaron once told me he got kicked out of the Marine Corps," Danny said suddenly.

"Is that good news or bad?" Toby said.

"I don't know. All I know is, in prison—" Danny stopped short.

"What?"

"Nothing," Danny mumbled.

Nick tilted the candle again. There was a way to read the future in the splattering of wax. *Ceromancy*, that was the word.

Through the window he saw a flare of light and then a fireball traveled in a low arc toward the boat. Overhead he heard the crash of Buddy's shotgun. Nora woke with a muffled yelp.

Buddy peered into the dark, his night vision gone. He tried to remember the track of the flare that now lay burning on the sand not far from the *Lily*. Another fireball appeared, arching higher and falling onto the foredeck. Buddy shot into the darkness, broke the double barrel, and reloaded. As he clicked the gun shut, a billowing orange flower climbed the wheelhouse. The spilled diesel that soaked the deck was burning now with a crackling of thorns and oily black smoke that was a shade darker than the night.

Toby was on deck with the large fire extinguisher, spraying the fire with foam. Somewhere in the darkness a rifle cracked, and Toby ducked low but continued to spray. Nick appeared with a second extinguisher, but the wheelhouse itself had caught fire, the wood dried with age and salt and covered with many coats of paint. The rifle cracked again, but Nick stood upright spraying the wheelhouse till his canister was empty.

"More extinguishers," Nick shouted at Nora. "The engine room." Another fireball came out of the dark and smashed on the back deck.

Nick grabbed the deck bucket and filled it with saltwater and threw it at the burning wheelhouse.

Buddy swung down from the flying bridge just as Nora reappeared with two more fire extinguishers. He grabbed her by the shoulder and said, "I can't see a thing. Only one of them's shooting and he's out of reach. I'm gonna go over the bow, try to get closer."

"What do you want us to do?"

"Take the canoe if you have to, but if you get the fire out just sit tight. The tide's starting to lift her. As soon as she floats, start the engine and fall back."

"What about you?"

"Whatever you do, don't wait. I'll be okay." Buddy hurriedly stuffed his pockets full of shells. "Don't forget there's two of them." He darted forward along the starboard side.

Nick and Toby almost had the fire under control. Nora took her shotgun and crouched by the rail and began firing into the night, not aiming at anything. Another fireball appeared, but it fell in the water and drifted astern, still burning.

Looking at the afterdeck Nora realized the canoe was no longer there. And where was Danny?

In the bow Buddy lowered a mooring line from the cleat and swung quickly down the starboard side, away from the gunner. When his feet had purchase on the shelving sand, he let go of the line. The water was above his knees, deeper than he had expected. For balance he put his left hand on the ironbark guard that protected the bow planks. He could feel the small gouges and scrapes where the anchor had struck the ironbark each time it was winched home. The scars of time. He began to wade across the flats.

Aaron had dropped back to the skiff, well out of shotgun range. He looked at the *Lily* and cursed the dying flames; she should have burned to the waterline. Now he would have to board her. A cold rill of doubt seeped through him, but he shook it off—it would be like shooting fish in a barrel. He put down his rifle and picked up the shotgun. It would be more useful in close quarters, along with his .357. He started back toward the *Lily*, no time to waste now.

Buddy hunched low, trying to find form in the darkness. Waves of cold shook his spine. He tried to relax his muscles completely, to trick his body into feeling the cold as a warm glow. But that contended with the worm of fire that had been eating his guts the past year, a worm that burned but did not warm.

The night seemed less dark now, not from approaching dawn but from a lessening of the storm that had tamped the dark in place. He had tried to memorize the flats before nightfall. The bar on which they were aground had two crowns with a bit of salt creek meandering through it, a creek that Sven and Aaron would have to cross if they tried to reach the *Lily*.

Buddy thought of the shotgun openings at Hidden Falls, when a flare was lit to open the fishing. Sven could be pretty cagey about positioning his boat, feinting and bluffing, but the *Viking Hero* was always one of the boats that jumped the gun. When the time came, Sven had only one tactic—put the hammer down. But there had only been one gun firing in the dark, of that Buddy was sure. Was there only one of them out there, and if so, which one?

He heard the whir of the starter on the *Lily* and then the main started. She must have righted herself enough for them to start the engine, but it would still be a little time till she floated.

Danny fought the waves, paddling first on one side and then the other. The current swept him onto the bar, and the canoe turned sideways and swamped, but he jumped clear. He dragged the canoe ashore and dumped the water out of it. When the gunfire and flames started, he had panicked and grabbed the canoe, thinking only of saving his own skin. There was no way this fracas would end well for Daniel T. Sullivan, no matter who came out on top. If he wanted to keep his freedom and his skin, he would have to look out for himself.

He heard the faint click of metal against metal and began to cautiously walk that way. To his surprise he found his own skiff, beached on the sand, the wind knocking a swivel snap against the hull. He scanned the area but not a soul was visible.

Nick and Nora sat on the floor of the galley, below the level of the windows, the candle between them. Toby knelt at the door, peering out into the night. The *Lily* shifted slightly.

"You think she'll come off yet?" Nick asked.

"Soon," Toby said

"What about Buddy?"

"He said not to wait for him," Nora said. "But I don't know."

Toby shook his head. "I don't like it, but we gotta try. Nick, if you take the wheel on the flying bridge. I'll man the searchlight."

"Won't that give them a target?" Nick asked.

"Yeah, maybe." Toby thought for a moment. "But we'll need it if something happens. I'll take a gun."

"Nora," Nick said, "you stay down here and keep a lookout for Buddy." He wanted her away from any gunfire.

Toby stood up and looked around as if taking stock. "Where's Danny?"

Nora snorted. "Gone." She fluttered her hands like a bird taking flight.

Buddy saw a shadow moving on the *Lily's* flying bridge. Too soon, he said to himself. Give her five more minutes. The engine revved and he could see the stern of the *Lily* slew hard to port, the prop almost audibly digging sand, but the bow remained fast. The engine cut back to an idle.

Aaron waded carefully through the knee-deep water. When the engine roared he began to run, knowing that if the *Lily* floated free he would lose his chance. A rivulet of deeper water tripped him and he fell headlong, then clambered up the far side. A shotgun spoke from his left, out of the darkness of the flats, and Aaron swiveled in surprise. The *Lily's* spotlight clicked on and scanned the water; a cone of light tracked past him, then returned and caught him, the bright disk burning his eyes till he felt like a jacklighted deer. He dropped his shotgun and drew his .357, holding it in both hands, pointing it at the searchlight. Another gunshot came from the left and Aaron ducked sideways, dropping the pistol. He scrabbled in the sand and picked up the shotgun, but now a shot from the *Lily* shredded the water in front of him. Then the gun on the left fired again, and Aaron felt a surge of panic, a visceral belief that the unknown gunner was Sven, risen from the depths to seek revenge.

He turned and ran, the searchlight losing him. If only he could reach the skiff and his rifle, the game might not be lost yet. But when he reached the ledge of sand, the skiff was gone, nothing but a keel mark to show it had ever existed.

Aaron hesitated, then followed the line of footprints till he found the beached canoe. What was this? Fucking Boy Scout Camp? He had never been in a canoe in his life, but it was his only chance. He still had his shotgun. Even if the *Lily* floated they would have to anchor up and wait for daylight. But it would be better if he could board her now, while they were preoccupied with getting her off. He pushed the canoe into the water, climbed in, and picked up a paddle.

When the searchlight slipped off the running figure, Buddy snapped a last shot in that direction. There had been only one; what had happened to the other? Buddy turned back toward the *Lily*, but his feet were like dead stumps and he almost fell twice in the first few yards. The beam of light swept the flats again and then tilted down and settled on the *Lily's* stern. Buddy heard the engine rev and this time the *Lily* moved. He began to run but the water was chest deep now. The *Lily* was only a few feet away, and he flopped down and began to swim awkwardly but had to drop the shotgun. Damn, he thought, Milo's Browning.

The *Lily* began to slide by, the rail high above him. He shouted desperately, and instantly Nora was there, reaching down. He grabbed at the outstretched hand and almost pulled her over. "Nick!" she screamed. "Toby!"

Nick appeared and grabbed one of Buddy's arms, then got a hand on his shirt collar.

"Where's Toby?" Nora asked. She didn't think she had enough strength left to help.

"Engine room," Nick gasped. "The bilge alarm went off." He heaved with all his might and brought Buddy to where he could grab the rail, but Buddy was so cold he could do no more than hold on.

"The boat," Buddy gasped, "she's still in gear."

Nick leaned way over and grabbed Buddy's belt. "Take the wheel," he said to Nora and heaved till Buddy got a leg over the rail.

Nora ran for the flying bridge. When Nick had left the bridge, he had cut the throttle but had forgotten to take the boat out of gear, and with the rudder half over she was curving slowly back toward the shallows. Nora cranked the wheel hard over the other way, but nothing seemed to happen. With her heart in her throat, hoping she was doing the right thing, she put her in reverse and then pushed the throttle hard down. The stern kicked sharply away.

Aaron was in the middle of the channel, paddling hard. The *Lily* was drifting slowly backward, away from him, and he redoubled his efforts, leaning so far over that the canoe shipped water. Suddenly the *Lily*'s engine roared and her stern swerved sideways and headed toward him at full throttle. The canoe struck below the stern counter and before he could react, Aaron was in the water, clinging to the canoe, kicking hard. The *Lily* continued backward, as if she knew he was there, rolling the canoe under. Aaron lost his grip on the canoe and the turn of the bilge struck him across the back. He struggled to regain the surface but lost his bearings as the darkness below reached up and gathered him in. The *Lily*'s keel struck a final blow, and he let the last bubble of air escape with a bellow of eternal rage.

Buddy was at the wheel now, dripping wet and shaking. From somewhere out in the dark they heard the high whine of an outboard motor. Nick swung the searchlight till it caught the skiff, not that far away, headed for the open sea. Nick saw something familiar in the figure hunched at the tiller. Nora picked up her shotgun and fired at the skiff.

"Nora, it's Danny!" Nick shouted, but she pumped the gun and fired again.

In the skiff Danny juked away from the spotlight, caught a glimpse of sand to his right, and turned hard back. He heard a shotgun fire and he zigged like a waterbug, cranking the tiller one way and then the other, the stern skittering wildly. He had no idea what was going on aboard the *Lily*, but he was not about to wait to find out.

"It's Danny!" Nick shouted again. Nora fired, pumped, fired again, till the gun was empty.

"Goddamn it, I know who it is," she said as she fumbled for more shells. She tried to load the gun, but the shells kept falling from her trembling fingers to roll across the flying bridge.

"Easy," Nick said and put his arms around her. "He's gone now."

"He started it, Nick," she said into his shoulder. "He started all of it."

When the spotlight let go of him, Danny throttled back and waited for his night vision to return. Though the wind had slackened, he could see a faint line of breakers ahead: the melee of the Koknuk Flats—twisting channels and breaking waves. He opened the throttle again and headed that way. Treacherous waters ahead, but at least he was alone in an open skiff, the only place he belonged.

CHAPTER 25

The seemingly endless procession of
winter storms is responsible for the
dreary, gray skies and frequent rain
and snow.

—US Coast Pilot

Winter rain marked the surface of the cove where the *Lily* lay. It was cold and dark in the galley; plywood now covered both windows. On the port side, the wheelhouse had almost burned through and rain further darkened the charred wood.

Nora extended her hands over the oil stove, trying to warm herself. She remembered a long-ago morning in a logging camp, the rain loud on the trailer roof, Trish asleep in her crib. All alone. Nora shifted and a bit of broken glass crunched beneath her feet.

"Half flood we'll try to leave," Buddy said. The three men sat at the galley table, fully dressed in coats and hats, their hands curled around coffee mugs.

"What's Milo gonna say when he sees the *Lily?*" Nick asked.

"Maybe he'll have a fire sale," said Toby. "We can pick up some gear cheap."

"I don't know," Buddy said. "But I think I'm gonna lower my offer." They all laughed.

The laughter grated on Nora's nerves—locker-room banter after the game. What were they thinking? There would be a lot of questions when they reached town, but how could she offer an explanation when she had no idea what had happened, nor why. Danny Sullivan might know, but where was he?

Nora moved over to the galley door and looked out at the green hills, then walked out on the back deck. Nick watched her with a worried expression, but somehow they all sensed that nothing was out there. The game had been played to conclusion. Nora remembered their last opening on the outer coast—the sea had looked the same, the sky and the coastline were unchanged and yet some component of energy was missing. The summer's salmon run had passed by, and they all felt the emptiness. This morning had a similar feeling of valediction.

Nora looked toward shore. She was desperate to call Trish. Now she wanted the child to be born. She needed to find something of value she could cling to.

There was movement on the beach, and Nora flinched backward, afraid of gunfire, but it proved to be two deer, picking their way along the drift pile. Mist gray wraiths, more insubstantial than a dream. Another ripple of laughter came from the galley, and Nora moved over to the rail so she would not have to hear whatever the men were saying. Beyond the deer she could see the green canoe, upside down on the beach, stranded by the tide. How had it come to be there?

Nora looked down at the rain-troubled water, the mixing of fresh and salt. One fathom down there would be no sense of the rain, a little deeper yet and there would be no knowledge of the light. Impossible to know what went on beneath the surface.

One last time she heard the tap of footsteps receding overhead in the house in Petersburg; a sound that was something more than imaginary, but then the footsteps stopped, cut short. Nora knew she would never know exactly what had happened to Melody.

From the engine room came the hard clank of the starter solenoid and then the roar of the big Caterpillar engine. The deer looked toward the *Lily*, their ears pricked forward. One jumped a drift log and entered the woven dark of the forest. The other followed but stopped to look back over its shoulder before disappearing. Buddy was on the flying bridge, and the *Lily* turned slightly and headed down channel. Nora watched the vee of the *Lily*'s wake ripple away, across water like cloudy silver.

BIOGRAPHICAL NOTE

Tom McGuire came to Alaska with two college friends. Fifty years later, he still hasn't found reason to leave. He has worked as a salmon fisherman, carpenter, and North Slope oilfield worker. He and his wife have raised four children in a house they built on the banks of the Chilkoot River. Grizzly bears are frequent visitors. Tom has also paddled thousands of miles down (and up) northern rivers. He has published a book, *99 Days on the Yukon*, that describes a summer-long trip with legendary canoeist Charlie Wolf.